HICKORY DICKORY DOCK

AGATHA CHRISTIE is known throughout the world as the Queen of Crime. Her seventy-seven detective novels and books of stories have been translated into every major language, and her sales are calculated in tens of millions.

She began writing at the end of the First World War, when she created Hercule Poirot, the little Belgian detective with the egg-shaped head and the passion for order – the most popular sleuth in fiction since Sherlock Holmes. Poirot, fluffy Miss Marple and her other detectives have appeared in films, radio programmes and stage plays based on her books.

Agatha Christie also wrote six romantic novels under the pseudonym Mary Westmacott, several plays and a book of poems; as well, she assisted her archaeologist husband Sir Max Mallowan on many expeditions to the Near East.

Postern of Fate was the last book she wrote before her death in 1976, but since its publication two books Agatha Christie wrote in the 1940s have appeared: *Curtain: Poirot's Last Case* and *Sleeping Murder*, the last Miss Marple Book. Agatha Christie's *Autobiography* was published in 1977.

AGATHA CHRISTIE

Hickory
Dickory Dock

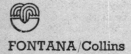

FONTANA/Collins

First published in 1955 by William Collins Sons & Co Ltd
First issued in Fontana Books 1958
Eleventh Impression March 1979

© 1955 by Max Edgar Lucien Mallowan
& William Edmund Cork

Made and printed in Great Britain by
William Collins Sons & Co Ltd, Glasgow

CHAPTER ONE

Hercule Poirot frowned.

'Miss Lemon,' he said.

'Yes, M. Poirot?'

'There are three mistakes in this letter.'

His voice held incredulity. For Miss Lemon, that hideous and efficient woman, never made mistakes. She was never ill, never tired, never upset, never inaccurate. For all practical purposes, that is to say, she was not a woman at all. She was a machine—the perfect secretary. She knew everything, she coped with everything. She ran Hercule Poirot's life for him, so that it, too, functioned like a machine. Order and method had been Hercule Poirot's watchwords from many years ago. With George, his perfect manservant, and Miss Lemon, his perfect secretary, order and method ruled supreme in his life. Now that crumpets were baked square as well as round, he had nothing about which to complain.

And yet, this morning Miss Lemon had made three mistakes in typing a perfectly simple letter, and moreover, had not even noticed those mistakes. The stars stood still in their courses!

Hercule Poirot held out the offending document. He was not annoyed, he was merely bewildered. This was one of the things that could not happen—but it had happened!

Miss Lemon took the letter. She looked at it. For the first time in his life, Poirot saw her blush; a deep ugly unbecoming flush that dyed her face right up to the roots of her strong grizzled hair.

'Oh, dear,' she said. 'I can't think how—at least, I *can*. It's because of my sister.'

'Your sister?'

Another shock. Poirot had never conceived of Miss Lemon's having a sister. Or, for that matter, having a father, mother or even grandparents. Miss Lemon, somehow, was so completely machine made—a precision instrument so to speak—that to think of her having affections, or anxieties, or family worries, seemed quite ludicrous. It was well known that the whole of Miss Lemon's heart and mind was given, when she was not on duty, to the perfection of a new filing system which was to be patented and bear her name.

'Your sister?' Hercule Poirot repeated, therefore, with an incredulous note in his voice.

Miss Lemon nodded a vigorous assent.

'Yes,' she said. 'I don't think I've ever mentioned her to you. Practically all her life has been spent in Singapore. Her husband was in the rubber business there.'

Hercule Poirot nodded understandingly. It seemed to him appropriate that Miss Lemon's sister should have spent most of her life in Singapore. That was what places like Singapore were for. The sisters of women like Miss Lemon married men in business in Singapore, so that the Miss Lemons of this world could devote themselves with machine-like effic-iency to their employers' affairs (and of course to the in-vention of filing systems in their moments of relaxation).

'I comprehend,' he said. 'Proceed.'

Miss Lemon proceeded.

'She was left a widow four years ago. No children. I managed to get her fixed up in a very nice little flat at quite a reasonable rent—'

(Of course Miss Lemon *would* manage to do just that almost impossible thing.)

'She is reasonably well off—though money doesn't go as far as it did, but her tastes aren't expensive and she has enough to be quite comfortable if she is careful.'

Miss Lemon paused and then continued:

'But the truth is, of course, she was lonely. She had never lived in England and she'd got no old friends or cronies and of course she had a lot of time on her hands. Anyway, she told me about six months ago that she was thinking of taking up this job.'

'Job?'

6

'Warden, I think they call it—or matron—of a hostel for students. It was owned by a woman who was partly Greek and she wanted someone to run it for her. Manage the catering and see that things went smoothly. It's an old-fashioned roomy house—in Hickory Road, if you know where that is.' Poirot did not. 'It used to be quite a superior neighbourhood once, and the houses are well built. My sister was to have very nice accommodation, bedroom and sitting-room and a tiny bath kitchenette of her own—'

Miss Lemon paused. Poirot made an encouraging noise. So far this did not seem at all like a tale of disaster.

'I wasn't any too sure about it myself, but I saw the force of my sister's arguments. She's never been one to sit with her hands crossed all day long and she's a very practical woman and good at running things—and of course it wasn't as though she were thinking of putting money into it or anything like that. It was purely a salaried position— not a high salary, but she didn't need that, and there was no hard physical work. She's always been fond of young people and good with them, and having lived in the East so long she understands racial differences and people's susceptibilities. Because these students at the hostel are of all nationalities; mostly English, but some of them actually *black*, I believe.'

'Naturally,' said Hercule Poirot.

'Half the nurses in our hospitals seem to be black nowadays,' said Miss Lemon doubtfully, 'and I understand much pleasanter and more attentive than the English ones. But that's neither here nor there. We talked the scheme over and finally my sister moved in. Neither she nor I cared very much for the proprietress, Mrs Nicoletis, a woman of very uncertain temper, sometimes charming and sometimes, I'm sorry to say, quite the reverse—and both cheese-paring and impractical. Still, naturally, if she'd been a thoroughly competent woman, she wouldn't have needed any assistance. My sister is not one to let people's tantrums and vagaries worry her. She can hold her own with anyone and she never stands any nonsense.'

Poirot nodded. He felt a vague resemblance to Miss Lemon showing in this account of Miss Lemon's sister—a Miss Lemon softened as it were by marriage and the climate of Singapore, but a woman with the same hard core of sense.

'So your sister took the job?' he asked.

'Yes, she moved into 26 Hickory Road about six months ago. On the whole, she liked her work there and found it interesting.'

Hercule Poirot listened. So far the adventure of Miss Lemon's sister had been disappointingly tame.

'But for some time now she's been badly worried. Very badly worried.'

'Why?'

'Well, you see, M. Poirot, she doesn't like the things that are going on.'

'There are students there of both sexes?' Poirot inquired delicately.

'Oh no, M. Poirot, I don't mean *that*! One is always prepared for difficulties of *that* kind, one *expects* them! No, you see, things have been disappearing.'

'Disappearing?'

'Yes. And such odd things . . . And all in rather an unnatural way.'

'When you say things have been disappearing, you mean things have been stolen?'

'Yes.'

'Have the police been called in?'

'No. Not yet. My sister hopes that it may not be necessary. She is fond of these young people—of some of them, that is —and she would very much prefer to straighten things out by herself.'

'Yes,' said Poirot thoughtfully. 'I can quite see that. But that does not explain, if I may say so, your own anxiety which I take to be a reflex of your sister's anxiety.'

'I don't like the situation, M. Poirot. I don't like it at all. I cannot help feeling that something is going on which I do not understand. No ordinary explanation seems quite to cover the facts—and I really cannot imagine what other

8

explanation there can be.'

Poirot nodded thoughtfully.

Miss Lemon's Heel of Achilles had always been her imagination. She had none. On questions of fact she was invincible. On questions of surmise, she was lost. Not for her the state of mind of Cortez' men upon the peak in Darien.

'Not ordinary petty thieving? A kleptomaniac, perhaps?'

'I do not think so. I read up the subject,' said the conscientious Miss Lemon, 'in the *Encyclopædia Britannica* and in a medical work. But I was not convinced.'

Hercule Poirot was silent for a minute and a half.

Did he wish to embroil himself in the troubles of Miss Lemon's sister and the passions and grievances of a polyglot hostel? But it was very annoying and inconvenient to have Miss Lemon making mistakes in typing his letters. He told himself that *if* he were to embroil himself in the matter, that would be the reason. He did not admit to himself that he had been rather bored of late and that the very triviality of the business attracted him.

' "The parsley sinking into the butter on a hot day," ' he murmured to himself.

'Parsley? Butter?' Miss Lemon looked startled.

'A quotation from one of your classics,' he said. 'You are acquainted, no doubt, with the Adventures, to say nothing of the Exploits, of Sherlock Holmes.'

'You mean these Baker Street societies and all that,' said Miss Lemon. 'Grown men being so silly! But there, that's men all over. Like the model railways they go on playing with. I can't say I've ever had time to *read* any of the stories. When I do get time for reading, which isn't often, I prefer an improving book.'

Hercule Poirot bowed his head gracefully.

'How would it be, Miss Lemon, if you were to invite your sister here for some suitable refreshment—afternoon tea, perhaps? I might be able to be of some slight assistance to her.'

'That's very kind of you, M. Poirot. Really very kind indeed. My sister is always free in the afternoons.'

'Then shall we say to-morrow, if you can arrange it?'

And in due course, the faithful George was instructed to provide a meal of square crumpets richly buttered, symmetrical sandwiches, and other suitable components of a lavish English afternoon tea.

CHAPTER TWO

Miss Lemon's sister, whose name was Mrs Hubbard, had a definite resemblance to her sister. She was a good deal yellower of skin, she was plumper, her hair was more frivolously done, and she was less brisk in manner, but the eyes that looked out of a round and amiable countenance were the same shrewd eyes that gleamed through Miss Lemon's pince-nez.

'This is very kind of you, I'm sure, M. Poirot,' she said. '*Very* kind. And such a delicious tea, too. I'm sure I've eaten far more than I should—well, perhaps just *one* more sand-wich—tea? Well, just *half* a cup.'

'First,' said Poirot, 'we make the repast—afterwards we get down to business.'

He smiled at her amiably and twirled his moustache, and Mrs Hubbard said:

'You know, you're exactly like I pictured you from Felicity's description.'

After a moment's startled realisation that Felicity was the severe Miss Lemon's Christian name, Poirot replied that he should have expected no less given Miss Lemon's effi-ciency.

'Of course,' said Mrs Hubbard absently, taking a second sandwich, 'Felicity has never cared for *people*. I do. That's why I'm so worried.'

'Can you explain to me exactly what does worry you?'

'Yes, I can. It would be natural enough for money to be taken—small sums here and there. And if it were jewellery that's quite straightforward too—at least, I don't mean straightforward, quite the opposite—but it would fit in—with kleptomania or dishonesty. But I'll just read you a list of the things that have been taken, that I've put down on paper.'

Mrs Hubbard opened her bag and took out a small note-book.

Evening shoe (one of a new pair)
Bracelet (costume jewellery)
Diamond ring (found in plate of soup)
Powder compact
Lipstick
Stethoscope
Ear-rings
Cigarette lighter
Old flannel trousers
Electric light bulbs
Box of chocolates
Silk scarf (found cut to pieces)
Rucksack (ditto)
Boracic powder
Bath salts
Cookery book

Hercule Poirot drew in a long deep breath.

'Remarkable,' he said, 'and quite—quite fascinating.'

He was entranced. He looked from the severe disapproving face of Miss Lemon to the kindly, distressed face of Mrs Hubbard.

'I congratulate you,' he said warmly to the latter.

She looked startled.

'But why, M. Poirot?'

'I congratulate you on having such a unique and beautiful problem.'

'Well, perhaps it makes sense to you, M. Poirot, but—'

'It does not make sense at all. It reminds me of nothing so much as a round game I was recently persuaded to play by some young friends during the Christmas season. It was called, I understand, the Three Horned Lady. Each person in turn uttered the following phrase, "I went to Paris and bought —" adding some article. The next person repeated that and added a further article and the object of the game was to memorise in their proper order the articles thus enumerated, some of them, I may say, of a most monstrous and ridiculous nature. A piece of soap, a white elephant, a gate-legged table and a Muscovy duck were, I remember, some of the items. The difficulty of the memorisation lay, of course, in the totally unrelated nature of the objects—the lack of sequence, so to speak. As in the list you have just shown me. By the time that, say, twelve objects had been mentioned, to enumerate them in their proper order became almost impossible. A failure to do so resulted in a paper horn being handed to the competitor and he or she had to continue the recitation next time in the terms, "I, a one horned lady, went to Paris," etc. After three horns had been acquired, retirement was compulsory, the last left in was the winner.'

'I'm sure you were the winner, M. Poirot,' said Miss Lemon, with the faith of a loyal employee.

Poirot beamed.

'That was, in fact, so,' he said. 'To even the most haphazard assembly of objects one can bring order, and with a little ingenuity, sequence, so to speak. That is : one says to oneself mentally, "With a piece of soap I wash the dirt from a large white marble elephant which stands on a gate-legged table"—and so on.'

Mrs Hubbard said respectfully : 'Perhaps you could do the same thing with the list of things I've given you.'

'Undoubtedly I *could*. A lady with her right shoe on, puts a bracelet on her left arm. She then puts on powder and lipstick and goes down to dinner and drops her ring in the soup, and so on—I could thus commit your list to memory—but it is not that we are seeking. Why was such a haphazard collection of things stolen ? Is there any system behind it ? Some fixed idea of any kind ? We have here primarily a process of analysis. The first thing to do is to study the list of objects very carefully.'

There was a silence whilst Poirot applied himself to study. Mrs Hubbard watched him with the rapt attention of a small boy watching a conjurer, waiting hopefully for a rabbit or at least streams of coloured ribbons to appear. Miss Lemon, unimpressed, withdrew into consideration of the finer points of her filing system.

When Poirot finally spoke, Mrs Hubbard jumped.

'The first thing that strikes me is this,' said Poirot. 'Of all these things that disappeared, most of them were of small value (some quite negligible) with the exception of two—a stethoscope and a diamond ring. Leaving the stethoscope aside for a moment, I should like to concentrate on the ring. You say a valuable ring—how valuable?'

'Well, I couldn't say exactly, M. Poirot. It was a solitaire diamond, with a cluster of small diamonds top and bottom. It had been Miss Lane's mother's engagement ring, I understand. She was most upset when it was missing, and we were all relieved when it turned up the same evening in Miss Hobhouse's plate of soup. Just a nasty practical joke, we thought.'

'And so it may have been. But I myself consider that its theft and return are significant. If a lipstick, or a powder compact or a book are missing—it is not sufficient to make you call in the police. But a valuable diamond ring is different. There is every chance that the police will be called in. So the ring is returned.'

'But why take it if you're going to return it?' said Miss Lemon, frowning.

'Why indeed,' said Poirot. 'But for the moment we will leave the questions. I am engaged now on classifying these thefts, and I am taking the ring first. Who is this Miss Lane from whom it was stolen?'

'Patricia Lane? She's a very nice girl. Going in for a what-do-you-call-it, a diploma in history or archæology or something.'

'Well off?'

'Oh no. She's got a little money of her own, but she's very careful always. The ring, as I say, belonged to her mother. She has one or two nice bits of jewellery but she doesn't have many new clothes, and she's given up smoking lately.'

'What is she like? Describe her to me in your own words.'

'Well, she's sort of betwixt and between in colouring. Rather washed out looking. Quiet and ladylike, but not much spirit or life to her. What you'd call rather a—well, an earnest type of girl.'

'And the ring turned up again in Miss Hobhouse's plate

of soup. Who is Miss Hobhouse?'

'Valerie Hobhouse? She's a clever dark girl with rather a sarcastic way of talking. She works in a beauty parlour. Sabrina Fair—I suppose you have heard of it.'

'Are these two girls friendly?'

Mrs Hubbard considered.

'I should say so—yes. They don't have much to do with each other. Patricia gets on well with everybody, I should say, without being particularly popular or anything like that. Valerie Hobhouse has her enemies, her tongue being what it is—but she's got quite a following too, if you know what I mean.'

'I think I know,' said Poirot.

So Patricia Lane was nice but dull, and Valerie Hobhouse had personality. He resumed his study of the list of thefts.

'What is so intriguing is all the different categories represented here. There are the small trifles that would tempt a girl who was both vain and hard up, the lipstick, the costume jewellery, a powder compact—bath salts—the box of chocolates, perhaps. Then we have the stethoscope, a more likely theft for a man who would know just where to sell it or pawn it. Who did it belong to?'

'It belonged to Mr Bateson—he's a big friendly young man.'

'A medical student?'

'Yes.'

'Was he very angry?'

'He was absolutely livid, M. Poirot. He's got one of those flaring up tempers—say anything at the time, but it's soon over. He's not the sort who'd take kindly to having his things pinched.'

'Does anyone?'

'Well, there's Mr Gopal Ram, one of our Indian students. He smiles at everything. He waves his hand and says material possessions do not matter—'

'Has anything been stolen from him?'

'No.'

'Ah! Who did the flannel trousers belong to?'

'Mr McNabb. Very old they were, and anyone else would

say they were done for, but Mr McNabb is very attached to his old clothes and he never throws anything away.'

'So we have come to the things that it would seem were not worth stealing—old flannel trousers, electric light bulbs, boracic powder, bath salts—a cookery book. They may be important, more likely they are not. The boracic was probably removed by error, someone may have removed a dead bulb and intended to replace it, but forgot—the cookery book may have been borrowed and not returned. Some charwoman may have taken away the trousers.'

'We employ two very reliable cleaning women. I'm sure they would neither of them have done such a thing without asking first.'

'You may be right. Then there is the evening shoe, one of a new pair, I understand? Who do they belong to?'

'Sally Finch. She's an American girl studying over here on a Fulbrite scholarship.'

'Are you sure that the shoe has not simply been mislaid? I cannot conceive what use one shoe could be to anyone.'

'It wasn't mislaid, M. Poirot. We all had a terrific hunt. You see Miss Finch was going out to a party in what she calls "formal dress"—evening dress to us—and the shoes were really vital—they were her only evening ones.'

'It caused her inconvenience—and annoyance—yes . . . yes, I wonder. Perhaps there is something there . . .'

He was silent for a moment or two and then went on.

'And there are two more items—a rucksack cut to pieces and a silk scarf in the same state. Here we have something that is neither vanity, nor profit—instead we have something that is deliberately vindictive. Who did the rucksack belong to?'

'Nearly all the students have rucksacks—they all hitch-hike a lot, you know. And a great many of the rucksacks are alike—bought at the same place, so it's hard to identify one from the other. But it seems fairly certain that this one belonged to Leonard Bateson or Colin McNabb.'

'And the silk scarf that was also cut about. To whom did that belong?'

'To Valerie Hobhouse. She had it as a Christmas present

—it was emerald green and really good quality.'

'Miss Hobhouse . . . I see.'

Poirot closed his eyes. What he perceived mentally was a kaleidoscope, no more, no less. Pieces of cut up scarves and rucksacks, cookery books, lipsticks, bath salts; names and thumb nail sketches of odd students. Nowhere was there cohesion or form. Unrelated incidents and people whirled round in space. But Poirot knew quite well that somehow and somewhere there must be a pattern. Possibly several patterns. Possibly each time one shook the kaleidoscope one got a different pattern. . . . But one of the patterns would be the right pattern. . . . The question was where to start. . . .

He opened his eyes.

'This is a matter that needs some reflection. A good deal of reflection.'

'Oh, I'm sure it does, M. Poirot,' assented Mrs Hubbard eagerly. 'And I'm sure I didn't want to trouble you—'

'You are not troubling me. I am intrigued. But whilst I am reflecting, we might make a start on the practical side. A start . . . The shoe, the evening shoe . . . yes, we might make a start there. Miss Lemon.'

'Yes, M. Poirot?' Miss Lemon banished filing from her thoughts, sat even more upright, and reached automatically for pad and pencil.

'Mrs Hubbard will obtain for you, perhaps, the remaining shoe. Then go to Baker Street Station, to the lost property department. The loss occurred—when?'

Mrs Hubbard considered.

'Well, I can't remember exactly now, M. Poirot. Perhaps two months ago. I can't get nearer than that. But I could find out from Sally Finch the date of the party.'

'Yes. Well—' He turned once more to Miss Lemon. 'You can be a little vague. You will say you left a shoe in an Inner Circle train—that is the most likely—or you may have left it in some other train. Or possibly a bus. How many buses serve the neighbourhood of Hickory Road?'

'Two only, M. Poirot.'

'Good. If you get no results from Baker Street, try Scotland Yard and say it was left in a taxi.'

'Lambeth,' corrected Miss Lemon efficiently.

Poirot waved a hand.

'You always know these things,'

'But why do you think—' began Mrs Hubbard.

Poirot interrupted her.

'Let us see first what results we get. Then, if they are negative or positive, you and I, Mrs Hubbard, must consult again. You will tell me then those things which it is necessary that I should know.'

'I really think I've told you everything I can.'

'No, no. I disagree. Here we have young people herded together, of varying temperaments, of different sexes. A loves B, but B loves C, and D and E are at daggers drawn because of A perhaps. It is all *that* I need to know. The interplay of human emotions. The quarrels, the jealousies, the friendships, the malice and all uncharitableness.'

'I'm sure,' said Mrs Hubbard, uncomfortably, 'I don't know anything about *that* sort of thing. I don't mix at all. I just run the place and see to the catering and all that.'

'But you are interested in people. You have told me so. You like young people. You took this post, not because it was of much interest financially, but because it would bring you in contact with human problems. There will be those of the students that you like and some that you do not like so well, or indeed at all, perhaps. You will tell me—yes, you will tell me! Because you are worried—not about what has been happening—you could go to the police about that—'

'Mrs Nicoletis wouldn't like to have the police in, I assure you.'

Poirot swept on, disregarding the interruption.

'No, you are worried about *someone*—someone who you think may have been responsible or at least mixed up in this. Someone, therefore, that you like.'

'Really, M. Poirot.'

'Yes, really. And I think you are right to be worried. For that silk scarf cut to pieces, it is not nice. And the slashed rucksack, that also is not nice. For the rest it seems childishness—and yet—I am not sure. No, I am not sure at all!'

CHAPTER THREE

Hurrying a little as she went up the steps, Mrs Hubbard inserted her latch key into the door of 26 Hickory Road. Just as the door opened, a big young man with fiery red hair ran up the steps behind her.

'Hallo, Ma,' he said, for in such fashion did Len Bateson usually address her. He was a friendly soul, with a Cockney accent and mercifully free from any kind of inferiority complex. 'Been out gallivanting?'

'I've been out to tea, Mr Bateson. Don't delay me now, I'm late.'

'I cut up a lovely corpse to-day,' said Len. 'Smashing!'

'Don't be so horrid, you nasty boy. A lovely corpse, indeed! The idea. You make me feel quite squeamish.'

Len Bateson laughed, and the hall echoed the sound in a great ha ha.

'Nothing to Celia,' he said. 'I went along to the Dispensary. "Come to tell you about a corpse," I said. She went as white as a sheet and I thought she was going to pass out. What do you think of that, Mother Hubbard?'

'I don't wonder at it,' said Mrs Hubbard. 'The idea! Celia probably thought you meant a *real* one.'

'What do you mean—a real one? What do you think our corpses are? Synthetic?'

A thin young man with long untidy hair strolled out of a room on the right, and said in a waspish way:

'Oh, it's only *you*. I thought it was at least a *posse* of strong men. The voice is but the voice of one man, but the volume is as the volume of ten.'

'Hope it doesn't get on your nerves, I'm sure.'

'Not more than usual,' said Nigel Chapman and went back again.

'Our delicate flower,' said Len.

'Now don't you two scrap,' said Mrs Hubbard. 'Good temper, that's what I like, and a bit of give and take.'

The big young man grinned down at her affectionately.

'I don't mind our Nigel, Ma,' he said.

A girl coming down the stairs at that moment said:

'Oh, Mrs Hubbard, Mrs Nicoletis is in her room and said she would like to see you as soon as you got back.'

Mrs Hubbard sighed and started up the stairs. The tall dark girl who had given the message stood against the wall to let her pass.

Len Bateson, divesting himself of his mackintosh said, 'What's up, Valerie? Complaints of our behaviour to be passed on by Mother Hubbard in due course?'

The girl shrugged her thin elegant shoulders. She came down the stairs and across the hall. 'This place gets more like a madhouse every day,' she said over her shoulder.

She went through the door at the right as she spoke. She moved with that insolent effortless grace that is common to those who have been professional mannequins.

Twenty-six Hickory Road was in reality two houses, 24 and 26 semi-detached. They had been thrown into one on the ground floor, so that there was both a communal sitting-room and a large dining-room on the ground floor, as well as two cloak-rooms and a small office towards the back of the house. Two separate staircases led to the floors above which remained detached. The girls occupied bedrooms in the right-hand side of the house, and the men on the other, the original No. 24.

Mrs Hubbard went upstairs loosening the collar of her coat. She sighed as she turned in the direction of Mrs Nicoletis's room.

She tapped on the door and entered.

'In one of her states again, I suppose,' she muttered.

Mrs Nicoletis's sitting-room was kept very hot. The big electric fire had all its bars turned on and the window was tightly shut. Mrs Nicoletis was sitting smoking on a sofa surrounded by a lot of rather dirty silk and velvet sofa cushions. She was a big dark woman, still good looking, with a bad-tempered mouth and enormous brown eyes.

'Ah! So there you are.' Mrs Nicoletis made it sound like an accusation.

20

Mrs Hubbard, true to her Lemon blood, was unperturbed. 'Yes,' she said tartly, 'I'm here. I was told you wanted to see me specially.'

'Yes, indeed I do. It is monstrous, no less, monstrous!'

'What's monstrous?'

'These bills! Your accounts!' Mrs Nicoletis produced a sheaf of papers from beneath a cushion in the manner of a successful conjurer. 'What are we feeding these miserable students on? *Foie gras* and quails? Is this the Ritz? Who do they think they are, these students?'

'Young people with a healthy appetite,' said Mrs Hubbard. 'They get a good breakfast and a decent evening meal —plain food but nourishing. It all works out very economically.'

'Economically? Economically? You dare to say that to me? When I am being ruined?'

'You make a very substantial profit, Mrs Nicoletis, out of this place. For students, the rates are on the high side.'

'But am I not always full? Do I ever have a vacancy that is not applied for three times over? Am I not sent students by the British Council, by London University Lodging Board—by the Embassies—by the French Lycée? Are not there always three applications for every vacancy?'

'That's very largely because the meals here are appetising and sufficient. Young people must be properly fed.'

'Bah! These totals are scandalous. It is that Italian cook and her husband. They swindle you over the food.'

'Oh no, they don't, Mrs Nicoletis. I can assure you that no foreigner is going to put anything over on *me*.'

'Then it is you yourself—*you* who are robbing me.'

Mrs Hubbard remained unperturbed.

'I can't allow you to say things like that,' she said, in the voice an old-fashioned Nanny might have used to a particularly truculent charge. 'It isn't a nice thing to do, and one of these days it will land you in trouble.'

'Ah!' Mrs Nicoletis threw the sheaf of bills dramatically up in the air whence they fluttered to the ground in all directions. Mrs Hubbard bent and picked them up, pursing her lips. 'You enrage me,' shouted her employer.

'I dare say,' said Mrs Hubbard, 'but it's bad for you, you know, getting all worked up. Tempers are bad for the blood pressure.'

'You admit that these totals are higher than those of last week?'

'Of course they are. There's been some very good cut price stuff going at Lampson's Stores. I've taken advantage of it. Next week's totals will be below average.'

Mrs Nicoletis looked sulky.

'You explain everything so plausibly.'

'There.' Mrs Hubbard put the bills in a neat pile on the table. 'Anything else?'

'The American girl, Sally Finch, she talks of leaving—I do not want her to go. She is a Fulbrite scholar. She will bring here other Fulbrite scholars. She must not leave.'

'What's her reason for leaving?'

Mrs Nicoletis humped monumental shoulders.

'How can I remember? It was not genuine. I could tell *that*. I always know.'

Mrs Hubbard nodded thoughtfully. She was inclined to believe Mrs Nicoletis on that point.

'Sally hasn't said anything to me,' she said.

'But you will talk to her?'

'Yes, of course.'

'And if it is these coloured students, these Indians, these Negresses—then they can all go, you understand? The colour bar, it means everything to these Americans—and for me it is the Americans that matter—as for these coloured ones—scram!'

She made a dramatic gesture.

'Not while I'm in charge,' said Mrs Hubbard coldly. 'And anyway, you're wrong. There's no feeling of that sort here amongst the students, and Sally certainly isn't like that. She and Mr Akibombo have lunch together quite often, and nobody could be blacker than he is.'

'Then it is Communists—you know what the Americans are about Communists. Nigel Chapman now—*he* is a Communist.'

'I doubt it.'

'Yes, yes. You should have heard what he was saying the other evening.'

'Nigel will say anything to annoy people. He is very tiresome that way.'

'You know them all so well. Dear Mrs Hubbard, you are wonderful! I say to myself again and again—what should I do without Mrs Hubbard? I rely on you *utterly*. You are a wonderful, wonderful woman.'

'After the powder, the jam,' said Mrs Hubbard.

'What is that?'

'Don't worry. I'll do what I can.'

She left the room, cutting short a gushing speech of thanks.

Muttering to herself: 'Wasting my time—what a maddening woman she is!' she hurried along the passage and into her own sitting-room.

But there was to be no peace for Mrs Hubbard as yet. A tall figure rose to her feet as Mrs Hubbard entered and said:

'I should be glad to speak to you for a few minutes, please.'

'Of course, Elizabeth.'

Mrs Hubbard was rather surprised. Elizabeth Johnston was a girl from the West Indies who was studying law. She was a hard worker, ambitious, who kept very much to herself. She had always seemed particularly well balanced and competent, and Mrs Hubbard had always regarded her as one of the most satisfactory students in the hostel.

She was perfectly controlled now, but Mrs Hubbard caught the slight tremor in her voice although the dark features were quite impassive.

'Is something the matter?'

'Yes. Will you come with me to my room, please?'

'Just a moment.' Mrs Hubbard threw off her coat and gloves and then followed the girl out of the room and up the next flight of stairs. The girl had a room on the top floor. She opened the door and went across to a table near the window.

'Here are the notes of my work,' she said. 'This represents several months of hard study. You see what has been done?'

Mrs Hubbard caught her breath with a slight gasp.

Ink had been spilled on the table. It had run all over the papers, soaking them through. Mrs Hubbard touched it with her fingertip. It was still wet.

She said, knowing the question to be foolish as she asked it:

'You didn't spill the ink yourself?'

'No. It was done whilst I was out.'

'Mrs Biggs, do you think—'

Mrs Biggs was the cleaning woman who looked after the top-floor bedrooms.

'It was not Mrs Biggs. It was not even my own ink. That is here on the shelf by my bed. It has not been touched. It was done by someone who brought ink here and did it deliberately.'

Mrs Hubbard was shocked.

'What a very wicked—and cruel thing to do.'

'Yes, it is a bad thing.'

The girl spoke quite quietly, but Mrs Hubbard did not make the mistake of underrating her feelings.

'Well, Elizabeth, I hardly know what to say. I am shocked, badly shocked, and I shall do my utmost to find out who did this wicked malicious thing. You've no ideas yourself as to that?'

The girl replied at once.

'This is green ink, you saw that.'

'Yes, I noticed that.'

'It is not very common, this green ink. I know one person here who uses it. Nigel Chapman.'

'Nigel? Do you think Nigel would do a thing like that?'

'I should not have thought so—no. But he writes his letters and his notes with green ink.'

'I shall have to ask a lot of questions. I'm very sorry, Elizabeth, that such a thing should happen in this house and I can only tell you that I shall do my best to get to the bottom of it.'

'Thank you, Mrs Hubbard. There have been—other things,

have there not?'

'Yes—er—yes.'

Mrs Hubbard left the room and started towards the stairs. But she stopped suddenly before proceeding down and instead went along the passage to a door at the end of the corridor. She knocked and the voice of Miss Sally Finch bade her enter.

The room was a pleasant one and Sally Finch herself, a cheerful redhead, was a pleasant person.

She was writing on a pad and looked up with a bulging cheek. She held out an open box of sweets and said indistinctly:

'Candy from home. Have some.'

'Thank you, Sally. Not just now. I'm rather upset.' She paused. 'Have you heard what's happened to Elizabeth Johnston?'

'What's happened to Black Bess?'

The nickname was an affectionate one and had been accepted as such by the girl herself.

Mrs Hubbard described what had happened. Sally showed every sign of sympathetic anger.

'I'll say that's a mean thing to do. I wouldn't believe anyone would do a thing like that to our Bess. Everybody likes her. She's quiet and doesn't get around much, or join in, but I'm sure there's no one who dislikes her.'

'That's what I should have said.'

'Well—it's all of a piece, isn't it, with the other things? That's why—'

'That's why what?' Mrs Hubbard asked as the girl stopped abruptly.

Sally said slowly:

'That's why I'm getting out of here. Did Mrs Nick tell you?'

'Yes. She was very upset about it. Seemed to think you hadn't given her the real reason.'

'Well, I didn't. No point in making her go up in smoke. You know what she's like. But that's the reason, right enough. I just don't like what's going on here. It was odd losing my shoe, and then Valerie's scarf being all cut to bits and Len's rucksack . . . it wasn't so much things being pinched—after all, that may happen any time—it's not nice but it's roughly normal—but this other isn't.' She paused for a moment, smiling, and then suddenly grinned. 'Akibombo's scared,' she said. 'He's always very superior and civilised—but there's a good old West African belief in magic very close to the surface.'

'Tchah!' said Mrs Hubbard crossly. 'I've no patience with superstitious nonsense. Just some ordinary human being making a nuisance of themselves. That's all there is to it.'

Sally's mouth curved up in a wide cat-like grin.

'The emphasis,' she said, 'is on ordinary. I've a sort of feeling that there's a person in this house who isn't ordinary!'

Mrs Hubbard went on down the stairs. She turned into the students' common-room on the ground floor. There were four people in the room. Valerie Hobhouse, prone on a sofa with her narrow, elegant, feet stuck up over the arm of it; Nigel Chapman sitting at a table with a heavy book open in front of him; Patricia Lane leaning against the mantelpiece, and a girl in a mackintosh who had just come in and who was pulling off a woolly cap as Mrs Hubbard entered. She was a stocky, fair girl with brown eyes set wide apart and a mouth that was usually just a little open so that she seemed perpetually startled.

Valerie, removing a cigarette from her mouth, said in a lazy drawling voice:

'Hallo, Ma, have you administered soothing syrup to the old devil, our revered proprietress?'

Patricia Lane said:

'Has she been on the warpath?'

'And how!' said Valerie and chuckled.

'Something very unpleasant has happened,' said Mrs Hubbard. 'Nigel, I want you to help me.'

'Me, ma'am?' Nigel looked up at her and shut his book. His thin, malicious face was suddenly illumined by a mischievous but surprisingly sweet smile. 'What have I done?'

'Nothing, I hope,' said Mrs Hubbard. 'But ink has been deliberately and maliciously spilt all over Elizabeth Johnston's notes, and it's green ink. You write with green ink, Nigel.'

He stared at her, his smile disappearing.

'Yes, I use green ink.'

'Horrid stuff,' said Patricia. 'I wish you wouldn't, Nigel. I've always told you I think it's horribly affected of you.'

'I like being affected,' said Nigel. 'Lilac ink would be even better, I think. I must try and get some. But are you serious, Mum? About the sabotage, I mean?'

'Yes, I *am* serious. Was it your doing, Nigel?'

'No, of course not. I like annoying people, as you know, but I'd never do a filthy trick like that—and certainly not to Black Bess who minds her own business in a way that's an example to some people I could mention. Where is that ink of mine? I filled my pen yesterday evening, I remember. I usually keep it on the shelf over there.' He sprang up and went across the room. 'Here it is.' He picked the bottle up, then whistled. 'You're right. The bottle's nearly empty. It should be practically full.'

The girl in the mackintosh gave a little gasp.

'Oh dear,' she said. 'Oh dear. I don't like it—'

Nigel wheeled at her accusingly.

'Have you got an alibi, Celia?' he said menacingly.

The girl gave a gasp.

'I didn't do it. I really didn't do it. Anyway, I've been at the hospital all day. I couldn't—'

'Now, Nigel,' said Mrs Hubbard. 'Don't tease Celia.'

Patricia Lane said angrily:

'I don't see why Nigel should be suspected. Just because *his* ink was taken—'

Valerie said cattishly:

'That's right, darling, defend your young.'

'But it's so unfair—'

'But really *I* didn't have anything to do with it,' Celia protested earnestly.

'Nobody thinks you did, infant,' said Valerie impatiently. 'All the same, you know,' her eyes met Mrs Hubbard's and exchanged a glance, 'all this is getting beyond a joke. Something will have to be done about it.'

'Something is going to be done,' said Mrs Hubbard grimly.

CHAPTER FOUR

'Here you are, M. Poirot.'

Miss Lemon laid a small brown paper parcel before Poirot. He removed the paper and looked appraisingly at a well-cut silver evening shoe.

'It was at Baker Street just as you said.'

'That has saved us trouble,' said Poirot. 'Also it confirms my ideas.'

'Quite,' said Miss Lemon, who was sublimely incurious by nature.

She was, however, susceptible to the claims of family affection. She said:

'If it is not troubling you too much, M. Poirot, I received a letter from my sister. There have been some new developments.'

'You permit that I read it?'

She handed it to him and after reading it, he directed Miss Lemon to get her sister on the telephone. Presently Miss Lemon indicated that the connection had been obtained. Poirot took the receiver.

'Mrs Hubbard?'

'Oh yes, M. Poirot. So kind of you to ring me up so promptly. I was really very—'

Poirot interrupted her.

'Where are you speaking from?'

'Why—from 26 Hickory Road, of course. Oh I see what you mean. I am in my own sitting-room.'

'There is an extension?'

'This is the extension. The main phone is downstairs in the hall.'

'Who is in the house who might listen in?'

'All the students are out at this time of day. The cook is out marketing Geronimo, her husband, understands very little English There is a cleaning woman, but she is deaf and I'm quite sure wouldn't bother to listen in.'

'Very good, then. I can speak freely. Do you occasionally have lectures in the evening, or films? Entertainments of some kind?'

'We do have lectures occasionally. Miss Baltrout, the explorer, came not long ago, with her coloured transparencies. And we had an appeal for Far Eastern Missions, though I am afraid quite a lot of the students went out that night.'

'Ah. Then this evening you will have prevailed on M. Hercule Poirot, the employer of your sister, to come and discourse to your students on the more interesting of his cases.'

'That will be very nice, I'm sure, but do you think—'

'It is not a question of *thinking*. I am sure!'

That evening, students entering the common-room found a notice tacked up on the board which stood just inside the door.

M. Hercule Poirot, the celebrated private detective, has kindly consented to give a talk this evening on the theory and practice of successful detection, with an account of certain celebrated criminal cases.

Returning students made varied comments on this.

'Who's this private eye?' 'Never heard of him.' 'Oh, I have. There was a man who was condemned to death for the murder of a charwoman and this detective got him off at the last moment by finding the real person.' 'Sounds crummy to me.' 'I think it might be rather fun.' 'Colin ought to enjoy it. He's mad on criminal psychology.' 'I would not put it precisely like that, but I'll not deny that a man who has been closely acquainted with criminals might be interesting to interrogate.'

Dinner was at seven-thirty and most of the students were already seated when Mrs Hubbard came down from her sitting-room (where sherry had been served to the distinguished guest) followed by a small elderly man with suspiciously black hair and a moustache of ferocious proportions which he twirled contentedly.

'These are some of our students, M. Poirot. This is M. Hercule Poirot who is kindly going to talk to us after dinner.'

Salutations were exchanged and Poirot sat down by Mrs Hubbard and busied himself with keeping his moustaches out of the excellent minestrone which was served by a small active Italian manservant from a big tureen.

This was followed by a piping hot dish of spaghetti and meat balls and it was then that a girl sitting on Poirot's right spoke shyly to him.

'Does Mrs Hubbard's sister really work for you?'

Poirot turned to her.

'But yes indeed. Miss Lemon has been my secretary for many years. She is the most efficient woman that ever lived. I am sometimes afraid of her.'

'Oh I see. I wondered—'

'Now what did you wonder, mademoiselle?'

He smiled upon her in paternal fashion, making a mental note as he did so.

Pretty, worried, not too quick mentally, frightened . . .
He said:

'May I know your name and what it is you are studying?'

'Celia Austin. I don't study. I'm a dispenser at St Catherine's Hospital.'

'Ah, that is interesting work?'

'Well, I don't know—perhaps it is.' She sounded rather uncertain.

'And these others? Can you tell me something about them, perhaps? I understood this was a home for foreign students, but these seem mostly to be English.'

'Some of the foreign ones are out. Mr Chandra Lal and Mr Gopal Ram—they're Indians—and Miss Reinjeer who's Dutch—and Mr Achmed Ali who's Egyptian and frightfully political!'

'And those who are here? Tell me about these.'

'Well, sitting on Mrs Hubbard's left is Nigel Chapman. He's studying Medieval History and Italian at London University. Then there's Patricia Lane next to him, with the spectacles. She's taking a diploma in Archæology. The big red-headed boy is Len Bateson he's a medical and the dark girl is Valerie Hobhouse, she's in a beauty shop. Next to her is Colin McNabb—he's doing a post-graduate course in Psychiatry.'

There was a faint change in her voice as she described Colin. Poirot glanced keenly at her and saw that the colour had come up in her face.

He said to himself:

'So—she is in love and she cannot easily conceal the fact.'

He noticed that young McNabb never seemed to look at her across the table, being far too much taken up with his conversation with a laughing red-headed girl beside him.

'That's Sally Finch. She's American—over here on a Fulbrite. Then there's Genevieve Maricaud. She's doing English, and so is Rene Halle who sits next to her. The small fair girl is Jean Tomlinson—she's at St Catherine's too. She's a physiotherapist. The black man is Akibombo—he comes from West Africa and he's frightfully nice. Then there's Elizabeth Johnston, she's from Jamaica and she's studying law. Next to us on my right are two Turkish students who came about a week ago. They know hardly any English.'

'Thank you. And do you all get on well together? Or do you have quarrels?'

The lightness of his tone robbed the words of seriousness.

Celia said:

'Oh, we're all too busy really to have fights, although—'

'Although what, Miss Austin?'

'Well—Nigel—next to Mrs Hubbard. He likes stirring people up and making them angry. And Len Bateson *gets* angry. He gets wild with rage sometimes. But he's very sweet really.'

'And Colin McNabb—does he too get annoyed?'

'Oh no. Colin just raises his eyebrows and looks amused.'

'I see. And the young ladies, do you have your quarrels?'

'Oh no, we all get on very well. Genevieve has feelings sometimes. I think French people are inclined to be touchy —oh, I mean—I'm sorry—'

Celia was the picture of confusion.

'Me, I am Belgian,' said Poirot solemnly. He went on quickly, before Celia could recover control of herself: 'What did you mean just now, Miss Austin, when you said that you wondered. You wondered—what?'

She crumbled her bread nervously.

'Oh that—nothing—nothing really—just, there have been some silly practical jokes lately—I thought Mrs Hubbard—But really, it was silly of me. I didn't mean anything.'

Poirot did not press her. He turned away to Mrs Hubbard and was presently engaged in a three-cornered conversation with her and with Nigel Chapman, who introduced the controversial challenge that crime was a form of creative art—and that the misfits of society were really the police who only entered that profession because of their secret sadism. Poirot was amused to note that the anxious looking young woman in spectacles who sat beside him tried desperately to explain away his remarks as fast as he made them. Nigel, however, took absolutely no notice of her.

Mrs Hubbard looked benignantly amused.

'All you young people nowadays think of nothing but politics and psychology,' she said. 'When I was a girl we were much more lighthearted. We danced. If you rolled back the carpet in the common-room there's quite a good floor, and you could dance to the wireless, but you never do.'

Celia laughed and said with a tinge of malice:

'But you used to dance, Nigel. I've danced with you myself once, though I don't expect you remember.'

'You've danced with *me*,' said Nigel incredulously. 'Where?'

'At Cambridge—in May Week.'

'Oh, May Week!' Nigel waved away the follies of youth. 'One goes through that adolescent phase. Mercifully it soon passes.'

Nigel was clearly not much more than twenty-five now. Poirot concealed a smile in his moustache.

Patricia Lane said earnestly:

'You see, Mrs Hubbard, there is so much study to be done. With lectures to attend and one's notes to write up, there's really no time for anything but what is really worth while.'

'Well, my dear, one's only young once,' said Mrs Hubbard.

A chocolate pudding succeeded the spaghetti and afterwards they all went into the common-room, and helped themselves to coffee from an urn that stood on a table. Poirot was then invited to begin his discourse. The two Turks politely excused themselves. The rest seated themselves and looked expectant.

Poirot rose to his feet and spoke with his usual aplomb. The sound of his own voice was always pleasant to him, and he spoke for three-quarters of an hour in a light and amusing fashion, recalling those of his experiences that lent themselves to an agreeable exaggeration. If he managed to suggest, in a subtle fashion, that he was, perhaps, something of a mountebank, it was not too obviously contrived.

'And so, you see,' he finished, 'I say to this city gentleman that I am reminded of a soap manufacturer I knew in Liége who poisoned his wife in order to marry a beautiful blonde secretary. I say it very lightly but at once I get a reaction. He presses upon me the stolen money I had just recovered for him. He goes pale and there is fear in his eyes. "I will give this money," I say, "to a deserving charity." "Do anything you like with it," he says. And I say to him then, and I say it very significantly, "It will be advisable, monsieur, to be *very* careful." He nods, speechless, and as I go out, I see that he wipes his forehead. He has had the big fright, and I—I have saved his life. For though he is infatuated with his blonde secretary he will not now try and poison his stupid and disagreeable wife. Prevention, always, is better than cure. We want to prevent murders— not wait until they have been committed.'

He bowed and spread out his hands.

'There, I have wearied you long enough.'

The students clapped him vigorously. Poirot bowed. And then, as he was about to sit down, Colin McNabb took his pipe from between his teeth and observed:

'And now, perhaps, you'll talk about what you're really here for!'

There was a momentary silence and then Patricia said reproachfully, 'Colin.'

'Well, we can all guess, can't we?' He looked round scornfully. 'M. Poirot's given us a very amusing little talk, but that's not what he came for. He's on the job. You don't really think, M. Poirot, that we're not wise to *that*?'

'You speak for yourself, Colin,' said Sally.

'It's true, isn't it?' said Colin.

Again Poirot spread out his hands in a graceful acknowledging gesture.

'I will admit,' he said, 'that my kind hostess has confided to me that certain events have caused her—worry.'

Len Bateson got up, his face heavy and truculent.

'Look here,' he said, 'what's all this? Has this been planted on us?'

'Have you really only just tumbled to *that*, Bateson?' asked Nigel sweetly.

Celia gave a frightened gasp and said: 'Then I *was* right!'

Mrs Hubbard spoke with decisive authority.

'I asked M. Poirot to give us a talk, but I also wanted to ask his advice about various things that have happened lately. Something's got to be done and it seemed to me that the only other alternative is—the police.'

At once a violent altercation broke out. Genevieve burst into heated French. 'It was a disgrace, shameful, to go to the police!' Other voices chimed in, for or against. In a final lull Leonard Bateson's voice was raised with decision.

'Let's hear what M. Poirot has to say about our trouble.'

Mrs Hubbard said:

'I've given M. Poirot all the facts. If he wants to ask any questions, I'm sure none of you will object.'

Poirot bowed to her.

'Thank you.' With the air of a conjurer he brought out a pair of evening shoes and handed them to Sally Finch.

'Your shoes, mademoiselle?'

'Why—yes—*both* of them? Where did the missing one come from?'

'From the Lost Property Office at Baker Street Station.'

'But what made you think it might be there, M. Poirot?'

'A very simple process of deduction. Someone takes a shoe from your room. Why? Not to wear and not to sell. And since the house will be searched by everyone to try and find it, then the shoe must be got out of the house, or destroyed. But it is not so easy to destroy a shoe. The easiest way is to take it in a bus or train in a parcel in the rush hour and leave it thrust down under a seat. That was my first guess and it proved right—so I knew that I was on safe ground—the shoe was taken, as your poet says, "to annoy, because he knows it teases".'

Valeria gave a short laugh.

'That points to you, Nigel, my love, with an unerring finger.'

Nigel said, smirking a little, 'If the shoe fits, wear it.'

'Nonsense,' said Sally. 'Nigel didn't take my shoe.'

'Of course he didn't,' said Patricia angrily. 'It's the most absurd idea.'

'I don't know about absurd,' said Nigel. 'Actually I didn't do anything of the kind—as no doubt we shall all say.'

It was as though Poirot had been waiting for just those words as an actor waits for his cue. His eyes rested thoughtfully on Len Bateson's flushed face, then they swept inquiringly over the rest of the students.

He said, using his hands in a deliberately foreign gesture:

'My position is delicate. I am a guest here. I have come at the invitation of Mrs Hubbard—to spend a pleasant evening, that is all. And also, of course, to return a very charming pair of evening shoes to mademoiselle. For anything further—' he paused. 'Monsieur—Bateson? yes, Bateson—has asked me to say what I myself think of this—trouble. But it would be an impertinence for me to speak unless I were invited so to do not by one person alone, but by you all.'

Mr Akibombo was seen to nod his black curled head in vigorous asseveration.

'That is very correct procedure, yes,' he said. 'True democratic proceeding is to put matter to the voting of all present.'

The voice of Sally Finch rose impatiently.

'Oh, shucks,' she said. 'This is a kind of party, all friends together. Let's hear what M. Poirot advises without any more fuss.'

'I couldn't agree with you more, Sally,' said Nigel.

Poirot bowed his head.

'Very well,' he said. 'Since you all ask me this question, I reply that my advice is quite simple. Mrs Hubbard—or Mrs Nicoletis rather—should call in the police *at once*. No time should be lost.'

CHAPTER FIVE

There was no doubt that Poirot's statement was unexpected. It caused not a ripple of protest or comment, but a sudden and uncomfortable silence.

Under cover of that momentary paralysis, Poirot was taken by Mrs Hubbard up to her own sitting-room, with only a quick polite 'Good night to you all,' to herald his departure.

Mrs Hubbard switched on the light, closed the door, and begged M. Poirot to take the arm-chair by the fireplace. Her nice good-humoured face was puckered with doubt and anxiety. She offered her guest a cigarette, but Poirot refused politely, explaining that he preferred his own. He offered her one, but she refused, saying in an abstracted tone: 'I don't smoke, M. Poirot.'

Then, as she sat down opposite him, she said, after a momentary hesitation:

'I dare say you're right, M. Poirot. Perhaps we *should* get the police in on this—especially after this malicious ink business. But I rather wish you hadn't said so—right out like that.'

'Ah,' said Poirot, as he lit one of his tiny cigarettes and watched the smoke ascend. 'You think I should have dissembled?'

'Well, I suppose it's nice to be fair and above board about things—but it seems to me it might have been better to keep quiet, and just ask an officer to come round and explain things privately to him. What I mean is, whoever's been doing these stupid things—well, that person's warned now.'

'Perhaps, yes.'

'I should say quite certainly,' said Mrs Hubbard rather sharply. 'No perhaps about it! Even if he's one of the servants or a student who wasn't here this evening, the word will get around. It always does.'

'So true. It always does.'

'And there's Mrs Nicoletis, too. I really don't know what attitude she'll take up. One never does know with her.'

'It will be interesting to find out.'

'Naturally we can't call in the police unless she agrees—oh, who's that now?'

There had been a sharp authoritative tap on the door. It was repeated and almost before Mrs Hubbard had called an irritable 'Come in,' the door opened and Colin McNabb, his pipe clenched firmly between his teeth and a scowl on his face, entered the room.

Removing the pipe, and closing the door behind him, he said:

'You'll excuse me, but I was anxious to just have a word with M. Poirot here.'

'With me?' Poirot turned his head in innocent surprise.

'Ay, with you.' Colin spoke grimly.

He drew up a rather uncomfortable chair and sat squarely on it facing Hercule Poirot.

'You've given us an amusing talk to-night,' he said indulgently. 'And I'll not deny that you're a man who's had a varied and lengthy experience, but if you'll excuse me for saying so, your methods and your ideas are both equally antiquated.'

'Really, Colin,' said Mrs Hubbard, colouring. 'You're extremely rude.'

'I'm not meaning to give offence, but I've got to make things clear. Crime and Punishment, M. Poirot—that's as far as your horizon stretches.'

'They seem to me a natural sequence,' said Poirot.

'You take the narrow view of the Law—and what's more, of the Law at its most old-fashioned. Nowadays, even the Law has to keep itself cognisant of the newest and most up-to-date theories of what *causes* crime. It is the *causes* that are important, M. Poirot.'

'But there,' cried Poirot, 'to speak in your new-fashioned phrase, I could not agree with you more!'

'Then you've got to consider the *cause* of what has been

happening in this house—you've got to find out why these things have been done.'

'But I am still agreeing with you—yes, that is most important.'

'Because there always is a reason, and it may be, to the person concerned, a very good reason.'

At this point, Mrs Hubbard, unable to contain herself, interjected sharply, 'Rubbish.'

'That's where you're wrong,' said Colin, turning slightly towards her. 'You've got to take into account the psychological background.'

'Psychological balderdash,' said Mrs Hubbard. 'I've no patience with all that sort of talk!'

'That's because you know precisely nothing about it,' said Colin, in a gravely rebuking fashion. He returned his gaze to Poirot.

'I'm interested in these subjects. I am at present taking a post-graduate course in psychiatry and psychology. We come across the most involved and astounding cases and what I'm pointing out to you, M. Poirot, is that you can't just dismiss the criminal with a doctrine of original sin, or wilful disregard of the laws of the land. You've got to have an understanding of the root of the trouble if you're ever to effect a cure of the young delinquent. These ideas were not known or thought of in your day and I've no doubt you find them hard to accept—'

'Stealing's stealing,' put in Mrs Hubbard stubbornly.

Colin frowned impatiently.

Poirot said meekly:

'My ideas are doubtless old-fashioned, but I am perfectly prepared to listen to you, Mr McNabb.'

Colin looked agreeably surprised.

'That's very fairly said, M. Poirot. Now I'll try to make this matter clear to you, using very simple terms.'

'Thank you,' said Poirot meekly.

'For convenience's sake, I'll start with the pair of shoes you brought with you to-night and returned to Sally Finch. If you remember, one shoe was stolen. Only one.'

'I remember being struck by the fact,' said Poirot.

Colin McNabb leaned forward; his dour but handsome features were lit up by eagerness.

'Ah, but you didn't see the *significance* of it. It's one of the prettiest and most satisfying examples anyone could wish to come across. We have here, very definitely, a *Cinderella complex*. You are maybe acquainted with the Cinderella fairy story.'

'Of French origin—*mais oui*.'

'Cinderella, the unpaid drudge, sits by the fire; her sisters, dressed in their finery, go to the Prince's ball. A Fairy Godmother sends Cinderella too, to that ball. At the stroke of midnight, her finery turns back to rags—she escapes hurriedly, leaving behind her *one slipper*. So here we have a mind that compares itself to Cinderella (unconsciously, of course). Here we have frustration, envy, the sense of inferiority. The girl steals a slipper. Why?'

'A girl?'

'But naturally, a girl. That,' said Colin reprovingly, 'should be clear to the meanest intelligence.'

'Really, Colin!' said Mrs Hubbard.

'Pray continue,' said Poirot courteously.

'Probably she herself *does not know why she does it*—but the *inner* wish is clear. She wants to be the Princess, to be identified by the Prince and claimed by him. Another significant fact, the slipper is stolen from an attractive girl *who is going to a ball.*'

Colin's pipe had long since gone out. He waved it now with mounting enthusiasm.

'And now we'll take a few of the other happenings. A magpie acquiring of pretty things—all things associated with attractive femininity. A powder compact, lipsticks, earrings, a bracelet, a ring—there is a two-fold significance here. The girl wants to be *noticed*. She wants, even, to be *punished*—as is frequently the case with very young juvenile delinquents. These things are none of them what you would call ordinary criminal thefts. It is not the *value* of these things that is wanted. In just such a way do well-to-do women go into department stores and steal things they could perfectly well afford to pay for.'

'Nonsense,' said Mrs Hubbard belligerently. 'Some people are just plain dishonest, that's all there is to it.'

'Yet a diamond ring of some value was amongst the things stolen,' said Poirot, ignoring Mrs Hubbard's interpolation.

'That was returned.'

'And surely, Mr McNabb, you would not say that a stethoscope is a feminine pretty pretty?'

'That had a deeper significance. Women who feel they are deficient in feminine attraction can find sublimation in the pursuit of a career.'

'And the cookery book?'

'A symbol of home life, husband and family.'

'And boracic powder?'

Colin said irritably:

'My dear M. Poirot. *Nobody* would steal boracic powder! Why should they?'

'This is what I have asked myself. I must admit, M. McNabb, that you seem to have an answer for everything. Explain to me, then, the significance of the disappearance of an old pair of flannel trousers—*your* flannel trousers, I understand.'

For the first time, Colin appeared ill at ease. He blushed and cleared his throat.

'I could explain that—but it would be somewhat involved, and perhaps—er well, rather embarrassing.'

'Ah, you spare my blushes.'

Suddenly Poirot leaned forward and tapped the young man on the knee.

'And the ink that is spilt over another student's papers, the silk scarf that is cut and slashed. Do these things cause you no disquietude?'

The complacence and superiority of Colin's manner underwent a sudden and not unlikeable change.

'They do,' he said. 'Believe me, they do. It's serious. She ought to have treatment—*at once*. But *medical* treatment, that's the point. It's not a case for the police. The poor little devil doesn't even know what it's all about. She's all tied up in knots. If I . . .'

Poirot interrupted him.

'You know then who she is?'

'Well, I have a very strong suspicion.'

Poirot murmured with the air of one who is recapitulating:

'A girl who is not outstandingly successful with the other sex. A shy girl. An affectionate girl. A girl whose brain is inclined to be slow in its reactions. A girl who feels frustrated and lonely. A girl . . .'

There was a tap on the door. Poirot broke off. The tap was repeated.

'Come in,' said Mrs Hubbard.

The door opened and Celia Austin came in.

'Ah,' said Poirot, nodding his head. 'Exactly. Miss Celia Austin.'

Celia looked at Colin with agonised eyes.

'I didn't know you were here,' she said breathlessly. 'I came—I came . . .'

She took a deep breath and rushed to Mrs Hubbard.

'Please, please don't send for the police. It's me. I've been taking those things. I don't know why. I can't imagine. I didn't want to. It just—it just came over me.' She whirled round on Colin. 'So now you know what I'm like . . . and I suppose you'll never speak to me again. I know I'm awful . . .'

'Och! not a bit of it,' said Colin. His rich voice was warm and friendly. 'You're just a bit mixed up, that's all. It's just a kind of illness you've had, from not looking at things clearly. If you'll trust me, Celia, I'll soon be able to put you right.'

'Oh, Colin—really?'

Celia looked at him with unconcealed adoration.

'I've been so dreadfully worried.'

He took her hand in a slightly avuncular manner.

'Well, there's no need to worry any more.' Rising to his feet he drew Celia's hand through his arm and looked sternly at Mrs Hubbard.

'I hope now,' he said, 'that there'll be no more foolish talk of calling in the police. Nothing's been stolen of any real worth, and what has been taken Celia will return.'

'I can't return the bracelet and the powder compact,' said Celia anxiously. 'I pushed them down a gutter. But I'll buy new ones.'

'And the stethoscope?' said Poirot. 'Where did you put that?'

Celia flushed.

'I never took any stethoscope. What should I want with a silly old stethoscope?' Her flush deepened. 'And it wasn't me who spilt ink all over Elizabeth's papers. I'd never do a—malicious thing like that.'

'Yet you cut and slashed Miss Hobhouse's scarf, mademoiselle.'

Celia looked uncomfortable. She said rather uncertainly:

'That was different. I mean—Valerie didn't mind.'

'And the rucksack?'

'Oh, I didn't cut that up. That was just temper.'

Poirot took out the list he had copied from Mrs Hubbard's little book.

'Tell me,' he said, 'and this time it must be the truth. What are you or are you not responsible for of these happenings?'

Celia glanced down the list and her answer came at once.

'I don't know anything about the rucksack, or the electric light bulbs, or boracic or bath salts, and the ring was just a mistake. When I realised it was valuable I returned it.'

'I see.'

'Because really I didn't mean to be dishonest. It was only—'

'Only what?'

A faintly wary look came into Celia's eyes.

'I don't know—really I don't. I'm all mixed up.'

Colin cut in in a peremptory manner.

'I'll be thankful if you'll not catechise her. I can promise you that there will be no recurrence of this business. From now on I'll definitely make myself responsible for her.'

'Oh, Colin, you are good to me.'

'I'd like you to tell me a great deal about yourself, Celia. Your early home life, for instance. Did your father and mother get on well together?'

'Oh no, it was *awful*—at home—'

'Precisely. And—'

Mrs Hubbard cut in. She spoke with the voice of authority.

'That will do now, both of you. I'm glad, Celia, that you've come and owned up. You've caused a great deal of worry and anxiety, though, and you ought to be ashamed of yourself. But I'll say this. I accept your word that you didn't spill ink deliberately on Elizabeth's notes. I don't believe you'd do a thing like that. Now take yourself off, you and Colin. I've had enough of you both for this evening.'

As the door closed behind them, Mrs Hubbard drew a deep breath.

'Well,' she said. 'What do you think of that?'

There was a twinkle in Hercule Poirot's eye. He said:

'I think—that we have assisted at a love scene—modern style.'

Mrs Hubbard made an ejaculation of disapproval.

'*Autres temps, autres mœurs*,' murmured Poirot. 'In my young days the young men lent the girls books on theosophy or discussed Maeterlinck's 'Bluebird.' All was sentiment and high ideals. Nowadays it is the maladjusted lives and the complexes which bring a boy and girl together.'

'All such nonsense,' said Mrs Hubbard.

Poirot dissented.

'No, it is not all nonsense. The underlying principles are sound enough—but when one is an earnest young researcher like Colin one sees nothing *but* complexes and the victim's unhappy home life.'

'Celia's father died when she was four years old,' said Mrs Hubbard. 'And she's had a very agreeable childhood with a nice but stupid mother.'

'Ah, but she is wise enough not to say so to the young McNabb! She will say what he wants to hear. She is very much in love.'

'Do you believe all this hooey, M. Poirot?'

'I do not believe that Celia had a Cinderella complex or that she stole things without knowing what she was doing. I think she took the risk of stealing unimportant trifles with

44

the object of attracting the attention of the earnest Colin McNabb—in which object she has been successful. Had she remained a pretty, shy, ordinary girl he might never have looked at her. In my opinion,' said Poirot, 'a girl is entitled to attempt desperate measures to get her man.'

'I shouldn't have thought she had the brains to think it up,' said Mrs Hubbard.

Poirot did not reply. He frowned. Mrs Hubbard went on:

'So the whole thing's been a mare's nest! I really do apologise, M. Poirot, for taking up your time over such a trivial business. Anyway, all's well that ends well.'

'No, no.' Poirot shook his head. 'I do not think we are at the end yet. We have cleared out of the way something rather trivial that was at the front of the picture. But there are things still that are not explained; and me, I have the impression that we have here something serious—really serious.'

Mrs Hubbard's face clouded over again.

'Oh, M. Poirot, do you really think so?'

'It is my impression . . . I wonder, madame, if I could speak to Miss Patricia Lane. I would like to examine the ring that was stolen.'

'Why, of course, M. Poirot. I'll go down and send her up to you. I want to speak to Len Bateson about something.'

Patricia Lane came in shortly afterwards with an inquiring look on her face.

'I am so sorry to disturb you, Miss Lane.'

'Oh, that's all right. I wasn't busy. Mrs Hubbard said you wanted to see my ring.'

She slipped it off her finger and held it out to him.

'It's quite a large diamond really, but of course it's an old-fashioned setting. It was my mother's engagement ring.'

Poirot, who was examining the ring, nodded his head.

'She is alive still, your mother?'

'No. Both my parents are dead.'

'That is sad.'

'Yes. They were both very nice people but somehow I was never quite so close to them as I ought to have been. One regrets that afterwards. My mother wanted a frivolous pretty daughter, a daughter who was fond of clothes and social things. She was very disappointed when I took up archæology.'

'You have always been of a serious turn of mind?'

'I think so, really. One feels life is so short one ought really to be doing something worth while.'

Poirot looked at her thoughtfully.

Patricia Lane was, he guessed, in her early thirties. Apart from a smear of lipstick, carelessly applied, she wore no make-up. Her mouse-coloured hair was combed back from her face and arranged without artifice. Her quite pleasant blue eyes looked at you seriously through glasses.

'No allure, *bon Dieu*,' said Poirot to himself with feeling. 'And her clothes! What is it they say? Dragged through a hedge backwards? *Ma foi*, that expresses it exactly!'

He was disapproving. He found Patricia's well-bred un-accented tones wearisome to the ear. 'She is intelligent and cultured, this girl,' he said to himself, 'and, alas, every year she will grow more boring! In old age—' His mind darted for a fleeting moment to the memory of the Countess Vera Rossakoff. What exotic splendour there, even in decay! These girls of nowadays—

'But that is because I grow old,' said Poirot to himself. 'Even this excellent girl may appear a veritable Venus to some man.' But he doubted that.

Patricia was saying:

'I'm really very shocked about what happened to Bess— to Miss Johnston. Using that green ink seems to me to be a deliberate attempt to make it look as though it was Nigel's doing. But I do assure you, M. Poirot, Nigel would never do a thing like that.'

'Ah.' Poirot looked at her with more interest. She had become flushed and quite eager.

'Nigel's not easy to understand,' she said earnestly. 'You see, he had a very difficult home life as a child.'

'*Mon Dieu*, another of them!'

'I beg your pardon?'

'Nothing. You were saying—'

'About Nigel. His being difficult. He's always had the

tendency to go against authority of any kind. He's very clever—brilliant really, but I must admit that he sometimes has a very unfortunate manner. Sneering—you know. And he's much too scornful ever to explain or defend himself. Even if everybody in this place thinks he did that trick with the ink, he won't go out of his way to say he didn't. He'll just say "Let them think it if they want to." And that attitude is really so utterly foolish.'

'It can be misunderstood, certainly.'

'It's a kind of pride, I think. Because he's been so much misunderstood always.'

'You have known him many years?'

'No, only for about a year. We met on a tour of the Châteaux of the Loire. He went down with flu which turned to pneumonia and I nursed him through it. He's very delicate and he takes absolutely no care of his own health. In some ways, in spite of his being so independent, he needs looking after like a child. He really needs someone to look after him.'

Poirot sighed. He felt, suddenly, very tired of love. . . . First there had been Celia, with the adoring eyes of a spaniel. And now here was Patricia looking like an earnest Madonna. Admittedly there must be love, young people must meet and pair off, but he, Poirot, was mercifully past all that. He rose to his feet.

'Will you permit me, mademoiselle, to retain your ring? It shall be returned to you to-morrow without fail.'

'Certainly, if you like,' said Patricia, rather surprised.

'You are very kind. And please, mademoiselle, be careful.'

'Careful? Careful of what?'

'I wish I knew,' said Hercule Poirot.

He was still worried.

CHAPTER SIX

The following day Mrs Hubbard found exasperating in every particular. She had awoken with a considerable sense of relief. The nagging doubt about recent occurrences was at last relieved. A silly girl, behaving in that silly modern fashion (with which Mrs Hubbard had no patience) had been responsible. And from now on, order would reign.

Descending to breakfast in this comfortable assurance, Mrs Hubbard found her newly attained ease menaced. The students chose this particular morning to be particularly trying, each in his or her way.

Mr Chandra Lal who had heard of the *sabotage* to Elizabeth's papers became excited and voluble. 'Oppression,' he spluttered, 'deliberate oppression of native races. Contempt and prejudice, colour prejudice. It is here well authenticated example.'

'Now, Mr Chandra Lal,' said Mrs Hubbard sharply. 'You've no call to say anything of that kind. Nobody knows who did it or why it was done.'

'Oh but, Mrs Hubbard, I thought Celia had come to you herself and really faced up,' said Jean Tomlinson. 'I thought it splendid of her. We must all be very kind to her.'

'Must you be so revoltingly pi, Jean?' demanded Valerie Hobhouse angrily.

'I think that's a very unkind thing to say.'

'Faced up,' said Nigel, with a shudder. 'Such an utterly revolting term.'

'I don't see why. The Oxford Group use it and—'

'Oh, for Heaven's sake, have we *got* to have the Oxford Group for breakfast?'

'What's all this, Ma? It is Celia who's been pinching those things, do you say? Is that why she's not down to breakfast?'

'I do not understand, please,' said Mr Akibombo.

48

Nobody enlightened him. They were all too anxious to say their own piece.

'Poor kid,' Len Bateson went on. 'Was she hard up or something?'

'I'm not really surprised, you know,' said Sally slowly. 'I always had a sort of idea . . .'

'You are saying that it was Celia who spilt ink on my notes?' Elizabeth Johnston looked incredulous. 'That seems to be surprising and hardly credible.'

'Celia did *not* throw ink on your work,' said Mrs Hubbard. 'And I wish you would all stop discussing this. I meant to tell you all quietly later but—'

'But Jean was listening outside the door last night,' said Valerie.

'I was not listening. I just happened to go—'

'Come now, Bess,' said Nigel. 'You know quite well who spilt the ink. I, said bad Nigel, with my little green phial, *I* spilt the ink.'

'He didn't. He's only pretending! Oh, Nigel, how can you be so stupid?'

'I'm being noble and shielding *you*, Pat. Who borrowed my ink yesterday morning? *You* did.'

'I do not understand, please,' said Mr Akibombo.

'You don't want to,' Sally told him. 'I'd keep right out of it if I were you.'

Mr Chandra Lal rose to his feet.

'You ask why is the Mau Mau? You ask why does Egypt resent the Suez Canal?'

'Oh, *hell*!' said Nigel violently, and crashed his cup down on his saucer. 'First the Oxford Group and now politics! At *breakfast*! I'm going.'

He pushed back his chair violently and left the room.

'There's a cold wind. Do take your coat.' Patricia rushed after him.

'Cluck, cluck, cluck,' said Valerie unkindly. 'She'll grow feathers and flap her wings soon.'

The French girl, Genevieve, whose English was as yet not equal to following rapid exchanges of English had been listening to explanations hissed into her ear by René. She now burst into rapid French, her voice rising to a scream.

'Comment donc? C'est cette petite qui m'a volé mon compact? Ah, par example! J'irai à la police. Je ne supporterai pas une pareille. . . .'

Colin McNabb had been attempting to make himself heard for some time, but his deep superior drawl had been drowned by the higher pitched voices. Abandoning his superior attitude he now brought down his fist with a heavy crash on the table and startled everyone into silence. The marmalade pot skidded off the table and broke.

'Will you hold your tongues, all of you, and hear me speak. I've never heard more crass ignorance and unkindness! Don't any of you have even a nodding acquaintance with psychology? The girl's not to be blamed, I tell you. She's been going through a severe emotional crisis and she needs treating with the utmost sympathy and care—or she may remain unstable for life. I'm warning you. The utmost care—that's what she needs.'

'But after all,' said Jean, in a clear, priggish voice, 'although I quite agree about being *kind*—we oughtn't to condone that sort of thing, ought we? Stealing, I mean.'

'Stealing,' said Colin. 'This wasn't *stealing*. Och! You make me sick—all of you.'

'Interesting case, is she, Colin?' said Valerie, and grinned at him.

'If you're interested in the workings of the mind, yes.'

'Of course, she didn't take anything of *mine*,' began Jean, 'but I do think—'

'No, she didn't take anything of yours,' said Colin, turning to scowl at her. 'And if you knew in the least what that meant you'd maybe not be too pleased about it.'

'Really, I don't see—'

'Oh, come on, Jean,' said Len Bateson. 'Let's stop nagging and nattering. I'm going to be late and so are you.'

They went out together. 'Tell Celia to buck up,' he said over his shoulder.

'I should like to make formal protest,' said Mr Chandra Lal. 'Boracic powder, very necessary for my eyes which much inflamed by study, was removed.'

'And you'll be late too, Mr Chandra Lal,' said Mrs Hubbard firmly.

'My professor is often unpunctual,' said Mr Chandra Lal gloomily, but moving towards the door. 'Also, he is irritable and unreasonable when I ask many questions of searching nature—'

'*Mais il faut qu'elle me le rende, compact,*' said Genevieve.

'You must speak English, Genevieve—you'll never learn English if you go back into French whenever you're excited. And you had Sunday dinner in this week and you haven't paid me for it.'

'Ah, I have not my purse just now. To-night—*Viens, René, nous serons en retard.*'

'Please,' said Mr Akibombo, looking round him beseechingly. 'I do not understand.'

'Come along, Akibombo,' said Sally. 'I'll tell you all about it on the way to the Institute.'

She nodded reassuringly to Mrs Hubbard and steered the bewildered Akibombo out of the room.

'Oh dear,' said Mrs Hubbard, drawing a deep breath. 'Why in the world I ever took this job on!'

Valerie, who was the only person left, grinned in a friendly fashion.

'Don't worry, Ma,' she said. 'It's a good thing it's all come out. Everyone was getting on the jumpy side.'

'I must say I was very surprised.'

'That it turned out to be Celia?'

'Yes. Weren't you?'

Valerie said in a rather absent voice:

'Rather obvious, really, I should have thought.'

'Have you been thinking so all along?'

'Well, one or two things made me wonder. At any rate she's got Colin where she wants him.'

'Yes. I can't help feeling that it's wrong.'

'You can't get a man with a gun,' Valerie laughed. 'But a spot of kleptomania does the trick? Don't worry, Mum. And for God's sake make Celia give Genevieve back her *compact*, otherwise we shall never have *any* peace at meals.'

Mrs Hubbard said with a sigh:

'Nigel has cracked his saucer and the marmalade pot is broken.'

'Hell of a morning, isn't it?' said Valerie. She went out. Mrs Hubbard heard her voice in the hall saying cheerfully:

'Good morning, Celia. The coast's clear. All is known and all is going to be forgiven—by order of Pious Jean. As for Colin, he's been roaring like a lion on your behalf.'

Celia came into the dining-room. Her eyes were reddened with crying.

'Oh, Mrs Hubbard.'

'You're very late, Celia. The coffee's cold and there's not much left to eat.'

'I didn't want to meet the others.'

'So I gather. But you've got to meet them sooner or later.'

'Oh, yes, I know. But I thought—by this evening—it would be easier. And of course I shan't stop on here. I'll go at the end of the week.'

Mrs Hubbard frowned.

'I don't think there's any need for that. You must expect a little unpleasantness—that's only fair—but they're generous minded young people on the whole. Of course you'll have to make reparation as far as possible—'

Celia interrupted her eagerly.

'Oh yes. I've got my cheque book here. That's one of the things I wanted to say to you.' She looked down. She was holding a cheque book and an envelope in her hand. 'I'd written to you in case you weren't about when I got down, to say how sorry I was and I meant to put in a cheque, so that you could square up with people—but my pen ran out of ink.'

'We'll have to make a list.'

'I have—as far as possible. But I don't know whether to try and buy new things or just to give the money.'

'I'll think it over. It's difficult to say off-hand.'

'Oh, but do let me give you a cheque now. I'd feel so much better.'

About to say uncompromisingly 'Really? And why should you be allowed to make yourself feel better?' Mrs Hubbard reflected that since the students were always short of ready cash, the whole affair would be more easily settled that way. It would also placate Genevieve who otherwise might make trouble with Mrs Nicoletis. (There would be trouble enough there anyway.)

'All right,' she said. She ran her eye down the list of objects. 'It's difficult to say how much off-hand—'

Celia said eagerly, 'Let me give you a cheque for what you think roughly and then you find out from people and I can take some back or give you more.'

'Very well.' Mrs Hubbard tentatively mentioned a sum which gave, she considered, ample margin, and Celia agreed at once. She opened the cheque book.

'Oh, bother my pen.' She went over to the shelves where odds and ends were kept belonging to various students. 'There doesn't seem to be any ink here except Nigel's awful green. Oh, I'll use that. Nigel won't mind. I must remember to get a new bottle of Quink when I go out.'

She filled the pen and came back and wrote out the cheque.

Giving it to Mrs Hubbard, she glanced at her watch.

'I shall be late. I'd better not stop for breakfast.'

'Now you'd better have something, Celia—even if it's only a bit of bread and butter—no good going out on an empty stomach. Yes, what is it?'

Geronimo, the Italian manservant, had come into the room and was making emphatic gestures with his hands, his wizened, monkey-like face screwed up in a comical grimace.

'The Padrona, she just come in. She want to see you.' He added, with a final gesture, 'She plenty mad.'

'I'm coming.'

Mrs Hubbard left the room while Celia hurriedly began hacking a piece off the loaf.

Mrs Nicoletis was walking up and down her room in a fairly good imitation of a tiger at the Zoo near feeding-time.

'What is this I hear?' she burst out. 'You send for the police? Without a word to me? Who do you think you are? My God, who does the woman think she is?'

'I did not send for the police.'

'You are a liar.'

'Now then, Mrs Nicoletis, you can't talk to me like that.'

'Oh no. Certainly not! It is *I* who am wrong, not *you*. Always *me*. Everything *you* do is perfect. Police in my respectable hostel.'

'It wouldn't be the first time,' said Mrs Hubbard, recalling various unpleasant incidents. 'There was that West Indian student who was wanted for living on immoral earnings and the notorious young Communist agitator who came here under a false name—and—'

'Ah! You throw that in my teeth? Is it my fault that people come here and lie to me and have forged papers and are wanted to assist the police in murder cases? And you reproach me for what I have suffered!'

'I'm doing nothing of the kind. I only point out that it wouldn't be exactly a novelty to have the police here—I dare say it's inevitable with a mixed lot of students. But the fact is that no one has "called in the police." A private detective with a big reputation happened to dine here as my guest last night. He gave a very interesting talk on criminology to the students.'

'As if there were any need to talk about criminology to our students! They know quite enough already. Enough to steal and destroy and sabotage as they like! And nothing is done about it—nothing!'

'I have done something about it.'

'Yes, you have told this friend of yours all about our most intimate affairs. That is a gross breach of confidence.'

'Not at all. I'm responsible for running this place. I'm glad to tell you the matter is now cleared up. One of the students has confessed that she has been responsible for most of these happenings.'

'Dirty little cat,' said Mrs Nicoletis. 'Throw her into the street.'

'She is ready to leave of her own accord and she is making full reparation.'

'What is the good of that? My beautiful Students' Home will now have a bad name. No one will come.' Mrs Nicoletis sat down on the sofa and burst into tears. 'Nobody thinks of my feelings,' she sobbed. 'It is abominable, the way I am treated. Ignored! Thrust aside! If I were to die to-morrow, who would care?'

Wisely leaving this question unanswered, Mrs Hubbard left the room.

'May the Almighty give me patience,' said Mrs Hubbard to herself, and went down to the kitchen to interview Maria.

Maria was sullen and unco-operative. The word 'police' hovered unspoken in the air.

'It is I who will be accused. I and Geronimo—the *povero*. What justice can you expect in a foreign land? No, I cannot cook the risotto as you suggest—they send the wrong rice. I make you instead the spaghetti.'

'We had spaghetti last night.'

'It does not matter. In my country we eat the spaghetti every day—every single day. The pasta, it is good all the time.'

'Yes, but you're in England now.'

'Very well then, I make the stew. The English stew. You will not like it but I make it—pale—pale—with the onions boiled in much water instead of cooked in the oil—and pale meat on cracked bones.'

Maria spoke so menacingly that Mrs Hubbard felt she was listening to an account of a murder.

'Oh, cook what you like,' she said angrily, and left the kitchen.

By six o'clock that evening, Mrs Hubbard was once more her efficient self again. She had put notes in all the students' rooms asking them to come and see her before dinner, and when the various summonses were obeyed, she explained that Celia had asked her to arrange matters. They were all, she thought, very nice about it. Even Genevieve, softened by a generous estimate of the value of her compact, said cheerfully that all would be *sans rancune* and added with a wise air, 'One knows that these crises of the nerves occur. She is rich, this Celia, she does not need to steal. No, it is a storm in her head. M. McNabb is right there.'

Len Bateson drew Mrs Hubbard aside as she came down when the dinner bell rang.

'I'll wait for Celia out in the hall,' he said, 'and bring her in. So that she sees it's all right.'

'That's very nice of you, Len.'

'That's O.K., Ma.'

In due course, as soup was being passed round, Len's voice was heard booming from the hall.

'Come along in, Celia. All friends here.'

Nigel remarked waspishly to his soup plate:

'Done *his* good deed for the day!' but otherwise controlled his tongue and waved a hand of greeting to Celia as she came in with Len's large arm passed round her shoulders.

There was a general outburst of cheerful conversation on various topics and Celia was appealed to by one and the other.

Almost inevitably this manifestation of goodwill died away into a doubtful silence. It was then that Mr Akibombo turned a beaming face towards Celia and, leaning across the table, said:

'They have explained me good now all that I did not understand. You very clever at steal things. Long time nobody know. Very clever.'

At this point Sally Finch, gasping out, 'Akibombo, you'll be the death of me,' had such a severe choke that she had to go out in the hall to recover. And the laughter broke out in a thoroughly natural fashion.

Colin McNabb came in late. He seemed reserved and even more uncommunicative than usual. At the close of the meal and before the others had finished he got up and said in an embarrassed mumble:

'Got to go out and see someone. Like to tell you all first. Celia and I—hope to get married next year when I've done my course.'

The picture of blushing misery, he received the congratulations and jeering cat-calls of his friends and finally escaped, looking terribly sheepish. Celia, on the other hand, was pink and composed.

'Another good man gone west,' sighed Len Bateson.

'I'm so glad, Celia,' said Patricia. 'I hope you'll be very happy.'

'Everything in the garden is now perfect,' said Nigel. 'Tomorrow we'll bring some *chianti* in and drink your health. Why is our dear Jean looking so grave? Do you disapprove of marriage, Jean?'

'Of course not, Nigel.'

'I always think it's so *much* better than free love, don't you? Nicer for the children. Looks better on their passports.'

'But the mother should not be too young,' said Genevieve. 'They tell one that in the physiology classes.'

'Really, dear,' said Nigel, 'you're not suggesting that Celia's below the age of consent or anything like that, are you? She's free, white, and twenty-one.'

'That,' said Mr Chandra Lal, 'is a *most* offensive remark.'

'No, no, Mr Chandra Lal,' said Patricia. 'It's just a—a kind of idiom. It doesn't mean anything.'

'I do not understand,' said Mr Akibombo. 'If a thing does not mean anything, why should it be said?'

Elizabeth Johnston said suddenly, raising her voice a little:

'Things are sometimes said that do not seem to mean anything but they may mean a good deal. No, it is not your American quotation I mean. I am talking of something else.' She looked round the table. 'I am talking of what happened yesterday.'

Valerie said sharply:

'What's up, Bess?'

'Oh, please,' said Celia. 'I think—I really do—that by tomorrow everything will be cleared up. I really mean it. The ink on your papers, and that silly business of the rucksack. And if—if the person owns up, like I've done, then everything will be cleared up.'

She spoke earnestly, with a flushed face, and one or two people looked at her curiously.

Valerie said with a short laugh:

'And we'll all live happy ever afterwards.'

Then they got up and went into the common-room. There was quite a little competition to give Celia her coffee. Then the wireless was turned on, some students left to keep appointments or to work and finally the inhabitants of 24 and 26 Hickory Road got to bed.

It had been, Mrs Hubbard reflected, as she climbed gratefully betwen the sheets, a long wearying day.

'But thank goodness,' she said to herself. 'It's all over now.'

CHAPTER SEVEN

Miss Lemon was seldom, if ever, unpunctual. Fog, storm, epidemic of flu, transport breakdowns—none of these things seemed to affect that remarkable woman. But this morning Miss Lemon arrived, breathless, at five minutes past ten instead of on the stroke of ten o'clock. She was profusely apologetic and for her, quite ruffled.

'I'm extremely sorry, M. Poirot—really extremely sorry. I was just about to leave the flat when my sister rang up.'

'Ah, she is in good health and spirits, I trust?'

'Well, frankly no.' Poirot looked inquiring. 'In fact, she's very distressed. One of the students has committed suicide.'

Poirot stared at her. He muttered something softly under his breath.

'I beg your pardon, M. Poirot?'

'What is the name of the student?'

'A girl called Celia Austin.'

'How?'

'They think she took morphia.'

'Could it have been an accident?'

'Oh no. She left a note, it seems.'

Poirot said softly, 'It was not this I expected, no, it was not this . . . and yet it is true, I expected *something*.'

He looked up to find Miss Lemon at attention, waiting with pencil poised above her pad. He sighed and shook his head.

'No, I will hand you here this morning's mail. File them, please, and answer what you can. Me, I shall go round to Hickory Road.'

Geronimo let Poirot in, and recognising him as the honoured guest of two nights before, became at once voluble in a sibilant conspiratorial whisper.

'Ah, signor, it is you. We have here the trouble—the big trouble. The little signorina, she is dead in her bed this morning. First the doctor come. He shake his head. Now comes an inspector of the police. He is upstairs with the signora and the padrona. Why should she wish to kill herself, the *poverina*? When last night all is so gay and the betrothment is made?'

'Betrothment?'

'*Si, si.* To Mr Colin—you know—big, dark, always smoke the pipe.'

'I know.'

Geronimo opened the door of the common-room and introduced Poirot into it with a redoublement of the conspiratorial manner.

'You stay here, yes? Presently, when the police go, I tell the signora you are here. That is good, yes?'

Poirot said that it was good and Geronimo withdrew. Left to himself, Poirot, who had no scruples of delicacy, made as minute an examination as possible of everything in the room with special attention to everything belonging to the students. His rewards were mediocre. The students kept most of their belongings and personal papers in their bedrooms.

Upstairs, Mrs Hubbard was sitting facing Inspector Sharpe, who was asking questions in a soft apologetic voice. He was a big comfortable looking man with a deceptively mild manner.

'It's very awkward and distressing for you, I know,' he said soothingly. 'But you see, as Dr Coles has already told you, there will have to be an inquest, and we have just to get the picture right, so to speak. Now this girl had been distressed and unhappy lately, you say?'

'Yes.'

'Love affair?'

'Not exactly.' Mrs Hubbard hesitated.

'You'd better tell me, you know,' said Inspector Sharpe, persuasively. 'As I say, we've got to get the picture. There was a reason, or she thought there was, for taking her own life? Any possibility that she might have been pregnant?'

'It wasn't that kind of thing at all. I hesitated, Inspector Sharpe, simply because the child had done some very foolish things and I hoped it needn't be necessary to bring them out in the open.'

Inspector Sharpe coughed.

'We have a good deal of discretion, and the coroner is a man of wide experience. But we have to *know*.'

'Yes, of course. I was being foolish. The truth is that for some time past, three months or more, things have been disappearing—small things, I mean—nothing very important.'

'Trinkets, you mean, finery, nylon stockings and all that? Money, too?'

'No money as far as I know.'

'Ah. And this girl was responsible?'

'Yes.'

'You'd caught her at it?'

'Not exactly. The night before last a—er—a friend of mine came to dine. A M. Hercule Poirot—I don't know if you know the name.'

Inspector Sharpe had looked up from his notebook. His eyes had opened rather wide. It happened that he did know that name.

'M. Hercule Poirot?' he said. 'Indeed? Now that's very interesting.'

'He gave us a little talk after dinner and the subject of these thefts came up. He advised me, in front of them all, to go to the police.'

'He did, did he?'

'Afterwards, Celia came along to my room and owned up. She was very distressed.'

'Any question of prosecution?'

'No. She was going to make good the losses, and everyone was very nice to her about it.'

'Had she been hard up?'

'No. She has an adequately paid job as a dispenser at St. Catherine's Hospital and has a little money of her own, I believe. She's rather better off than most of our students.'

'So she'd no need to steal—but did,' said the inspector, writing it down.

'It's kleptomania, I suppose,' said Mrs Hubbard.

'That's the label that's used. I just mean one of the people that don't *need* to take things, but nevertheless *do* take them.'

'I wonder if you're being a little unfair to her. You see, there was a young man.'

'And he ratted on her?'

'Oh no. *Quite* the reverse. He spoke very strongly in her defence and as a matter of fact, last night, after supper, he announced that they'd become engaged.'

Inspector Sharpe's eyebrows mounted his forehead in a surprised fashion.

'And then she goes up to bed and takes morphia? That's rather surprising, isn't it?'

'It is. I can't understand it.'

Mrs Hubbard's face was creased with perplexity and distress.

'And yet the facts are clear enough.' Sharpe nodded to the small torn piece of paper that lay on the table between them.

Dear Mrs Hubbard (it ran), *I really* am *sorry and this is the best thing I can do.*

'It's not signed, but you've no doubt it's her handwriting?'

'No.'

Mrs Hubbard spoke rather uncertainly and frowned as she looked at the torn scrap of paper. Why did she feel so strongly that there was something *wrong* about it—?

'There's one clear fingerprint on it which is definitely hers,' said the inspector. 'The morphia was in a small bottle with the label of St Catherine's Hospital on it and you tell me that she works as a dispenser in St Catherine's. She'd have access to the poison cupboard and that's where she probably got it. Presumably she brought it home with her yesterday with suicide in mind.'

'I really can't believe it. It doesn't seem right somehow. She was so happy last night.'

'Then we must suppose that a reaction set in when she went up to bed. Perhaps there's more in her past than you know about. Perhaps she was afraid of that coming out.

You think she was very much in love with this young man
—what's his name, by the way?'

'Colin McNabb. He's doing a post-graduate course at St
Catherine's.'

'A doctor? And at St Catherine's?'

'Celia was very much in love with him, more, I should
say, than he with her. He's a rather self-centred young man.'

'Then that's probably the explanation. She didn't feel
worthy of him, or hadn't told him all she ought to tell him.
She was quite young, wasn't she?'

'Twenty-three.'

'They're idealistic at that age and they take love affairs
hard. Yes, that's it, I'm afraid. Pity.'

He rose to his feet. 'I'm afraid the actual facts will have
to come out, but we'll do all we can to gloss things over.
Thank you, Mrs Hubbard. I've got all the information I
need now. Her mother died two years ago and the only
relative you know of is this elderly aunt in Yorkshire—we'll
communicate with her.'

He picked up the small torn fragment with Celia's agitated
writing on it.

'There's something wrong about that,' said Mrs Hubbard
suddenly.

'Wrong? In what way?'

'I don't know—but I feel I ought to know. Oh dear.'

'You're quite sure it's her handwriting?'

'Oh yes. It's not *that*.' Mrs Hubbard pressed her hands to
her eyeballs.

'I feel so dreadfully stupid this morning,' she said
apologetically.

'It's all been very trying for you, I know,' said the
inspector with gentle sympathy. 'I don't think we'll need
to trouble you further at the moment, Mrs Hubbard.'

Inspector Sharpe opened the door and immediately fell
over Geronimo, who was pressed against the door outside.

'Hallo,' said Inspector Sharpe pleasantly. 'Listening at
doors, eh?'

No, no,' Geronimo answered with an air of virtuous
indignation. 'I do not listen—never, never! I am just

coming in with message.'

'*I see. What message?*'

Geronimo said sulkily:

'Only that there is gentleman downstairs to see la Signora Hubbard.'

'All right. Go along in, sonny, and tell her.'

He walked past Geronimo down the passage and then, taking a leaf out of the Italian's book, turned sharply, and tiptoed noiselessly back. Might as well know if little monkey-face had been telling the truth.

He arrived in time to hear Geronimo say:

'The gentleman who came to supper the other night, the gentleman with the moustaches, he is downstairs waiting to see you.'

'Eh? What?' Mrs Hubbard sounded abstracted. 'Oh, thank you, Geronimo. I'll be down in a minute or two.'

'Gentleman with the moustaches, eh,' said Sharpe to himself, grinning. 'I bet I know who *that* is.'

He went downstairs and into the common-room.

'Hallo, M. Poirot,' he said. 'It's a long time since we met.'

Poirot rose without visible discomposure from a kneeling position by the bottom shelf near the fireplace.

'Aha,' he said. 'But surely—yes, it is Inspector Sharpe, is it not? But you were not formerly in this division?'

'Transferred two years ago. Remember that business down at Crays Hill?'

'Ah yes. That is a long time ago now. You are still a young man, Inspector—'

'Getting on, getting on.'

'—and I am an old one. Alas!' Poirot sighed.

'But still active, eh, M. Poirot. Active in certain ways, shall we say?'

'Now what do you mean by that?'

'I mean that I'd like to know *why* you came along here the other night to give a talk on criminology to students.'

Poirot smiled.

'But there is such a simple explanation. Mrs Hubbard here is the sister of my much valued secretary, Miss Lemon. So when she asked me—'

'When she asked you to look into what had been going on here, you came along. That's it really, isn't it?'

'You are quite correct.'

'But why? That's what I want to know. What was there in it for you?'

'To interest me, you mean?'

'That's what I mean. Here's a silly kid who's been pinching a few things here and there. Happens all the time. Rather small beer for you, M. Poirot, isn't it?'

Poirot shook his head.

'It is not so simple as that.'

'Why not? What isn't simple about it?'

Poirot sat down on a chair. With a slight frown he dusted the knees of his trousers.

'I wish I knew,' he said simply.

Sharpe frowned.

'I don't understand,' he said.

'No, and I do not understand. The things that were taken—' He shook his head. 'They did not make a pattern —they did not make sense. It is like seeing a trail of foot-prints and they are not all made by the same feet. There is, quite clearly, the print of what you have called "a silly kid"—but there is more than that. Other things happened that were meant to fit in with the pattern of Celia Austin— but they did *not* fit in. They were meaningless, apparently purposeless. There was evidence, too, of malice. And Celia was not malicious.'

'She was a kleptomaniac?'

'I should very much doubt it.'

'Just an ordinary petty thief, then?'

'Not in the way you mean. I give it you as my opinion that all this pilfering of petty objects was done to attract the attention of a certain young man.'

'Colin McNabb?'

'Yes. She was desperately in love with Colin McNabb. Colin never noticed her. Instead of a nice, pretty, well behaved young girl, she displayed herself as an interesting young criminal. The result was successful. Colin McNabb immediately fell for her, as they say, in a big way.'

'He must be a complete fool, then.'

'Not at all. He is a keen psychologist.'

'Oh,' Inspector Sharpe groaned. 'One of *those*! I understand now.' A faint grin showed on his face. 'Pretty smart of the girl.'

'Surprisingly so.'

Poirot repeated, musingly, 'Yes, surprisingly so.'

Inspector Sharpe looked alert.

'Meaning by that, M. Poirot?'

'That I wondered—I still wonder—if the idea had been suggested to her by someone else?'

'For what reason?'

'How do I know? Altruism? Some ulterior motive? One is in the dark.'

'Any idea as to who it might have been who gave her the tip?'

'No—unless—but no—'

'All the same,' said Sharpe, pondering, 'I don't quite get it. If she's been simply trying this kleptomania business on, *and* it's succeeded, why the hell go and commit suicide?'

'The answer is that she should *not* have committed suicide.'

The two men looked at each other.

Poirot murmured:

'You are quite sure that she did?'

'It's clear as day, M. Poirot. 'There's no reason to believe otherwise and—'

The door opened and Mrs Hubbard came in. She looked flushed and triumphant. Her chin stuck out aggressively.

'I've got it,' she said triumphantly. 'Good morning, M. Poirot. I've got it, Inspector Sharpe. It came to me quite suddenly. Why that suicide note looked wrong, I mean. Celia couldn't possibly have written it.'

'Why not, Mrs Hubbard?'

'Because it's written in ordinary blue black ink. And Celia filled her pen with green ink—that ink over there,' Mrs Hubbard nodded towards the shelf, 'at breakfast-time yesterday morning.'

Inspector Sharpe, a somewhat different Inspector Sharpe,

came back into the room which he had left abruptly after Mrs Hubbard's statement.

'Quite right,' he said. 'I've checked up. The only pen in the girl's room, the one that was by her bed, has green ink in it. Now that green ink—'

Mrs Hubbard held up the nearly empty bottle.

Then she explained, clearly and concisely, the scene at the breakfast table.

'I feel sure,' she ended, 'that the scrap of paper was torn out of the letter she had written to me yesterday—and which I never opened.'

'What did she do with it? Can you remember?'

Mrs Hubbard shook her head.

'I left her alone in here and went to do my housekeeping. She must, I think, have left it lying somewhere in here, and forgotten about it.'

'And somebody found it . . . and opened it . . . somebody—'

He broke off.

'You realise,' he said, 'what this means? I haven't been very happy about this torn bit of paper all along. There was quite a pile of lecture notepaper in her room—much more natural to write a suicide note on one of them. This means that somebody saw the possibility of using the opening phrase of her letter to you—to suggest something very different. To suggest suicide—'

He paused and then said slowly:

'This means—'

'Murder,' said Hercule Poirot.

CHAPTER EIGHT

Though personally deprecating *le five o'clock* as inhibiting the proper appreciation of the supreme meal of the day, dinner, Poirot was now getting quite accustomed to serving it.

The resourceful George had on this occasion produced large cups, a pot of really strong Indian tea and, in addition to the hot and buttery square crumpets, bread and jam and a large square of rich plum cake.

All this for the delectation of Inspector Sharpe, who was leaning back contentedly sipping his third cup of tea.

'You don't mind my coming along like this, M. Poirot? I've got an hour to spare until the time when the students will be getting back. I shall want to question them all—and, frankly, it's not a business I'm looking forward to. You met some of them the other night and I wondered if you could give me any useful dope—on the foreigners, anyway.'

'You think I am a good judge of foreigners? But, *mon cher*, there were no Belgians amongst them.'

'No Belg—oh, I see what you mean! You mean that as you're a Belgian, all the other nationalities are as foreign to you as they are to me. But that's not quite true, is it? I mean you probably know more about the Continental types than I do—though not the Indians and the West Africans and that lot.'

'Your best assistance will probably be from Mrs Hubbard. She has been there for some months in intimate association with these young people and she is quite a good judge of human nature.'

'Yes, thoroughly competent woman. I'm relying on her. I shall have to see the proprietress of the place, too. She wasn't there this morning. Owns several of these places, I understand, as well as some of the student clubs. Doesn't seem to be much liked.'

Poirot said nothing for a moment or two, then he asked:
'You have been to St Catherine's?'

'Yes. The chief pharmacist was most helpful. He was

much shocked and distressed by the news.'

'What did he say of the girl?'

'She'd worked there for just over a year and was well liked. He described her as rather slow, but very conscientious.' He paused and then added, 'The morphia came from there all right.'

'It did? That is interesting—and rather puzzling.'

'It was morphine tartrate. Kept in the poison cupboard in the Dispensary. Upper shelf—amongst drugs that were not often used. The hypodermic tablets, of course, are what are in general use, and it appears that morphine hydrochloride is more often used than the tartrate. There seems to be a kind of fashion in drugs like everything else. Doctors seem to follow one another in prescribing like a lot of sheep. He didn't say that. It was my own thought. There are some drugs in the upper shelf of that cupboard that were once popular, but haven't been prescribed for years.'

'So the absence of one small dusty phial would not immediately be noticed?'

'That's right. Stock-taking is only done at regular intervals. Nobody remembers any prescription with morphine tartrate in it for a long time. The absence of the bottle wouldn't be noticed until it was wanted—or until they went over stock. The three dispensers all had keys of the poison cupboard and the dangerous drug cupboard. The cupboards are opened as needed, and as on a busy day (which is practically every day) someone is going to the cupboard every few minutes, the cupboard is unlocked and remains unlocked till the end of work.'

'Who has access to it, other than Celia herself?'

'The two other women dispensers, but they have no connection of any kind with Hickory Road. One has been there for four years, the other only came a few weeks ago, was formerly at a hospital in Devon. Good record. Then there are the three senior pharmacists who have all been at St Catherine's for years. Those are the people who have what you might call rightful and normal access to the cupboard. Then there's an old woman who scrubs the floors. She's there between nine and ten in the morning and she could have grabbed a bottle out of the cupboard if the girls were busy at the outpatients' hatches, or attending to the ward baskets, but she's been working for the hospital for years and it seems very unlikely. The lab. attendant comes through with stock bottles and he, too, could help himself to a bottle if he watched his opportunity—but none of these suggestions seem at all probable.'

'What outsiders come into the Dispensary?'

'Quite a lot, one way or another. They'd pass through the Dispensary to go to the chief pharmacist's office for instance—or travellers from the big wholesale drug houses would go through it to the manufacturing departments. Then, of course, friends come in occasionally to see one of the dispensers—not a usual thing, but it happens.'

'That is better. Who came in recently to see Celia Austin?'

Sharpe consulted his notebook.

'A girl called Patricia Lane came in on Tuesday of last week. She wanted Celia to come to meet her at the pictures after the Dispensary closed.'

'Patricia Lane,' said Poirot thoughtfully.

'She was only there about five minutes and she did not go near the poison cupboard but remained near the outpatients' windows talking to Celia and another girl. They also remember a coloured girl coming—about two weeks ago—a very superior girl, they said. She was interested in the work and asked questions about it and made notes. Spoke perfect English.'

'That would be Elizabeth Johnston. She was interested, was she?'

'It was a Welfare Clinic afternoon. She was interested in the organisation of such things and also in what was prescribed for such ailments as infant diarrhœa and skin infections.'

Poirot nodded.

'Anyone else?'

'Not that can be remembered.'

'Do doctors come to the Dispensary?'

Sharpe grinned.

'All the time. Officially and unofficially. Sometimes to ask about a particular formula, or to see what is kept in stock.'

'To see what is kept in stock?'

'Yes, I thought of that. Sometimes they ask advice—about a substitute for some preparation that seems to irritate a patient's skin or interfere with digestion unduly. Sometimes a physician just strolls in for a chat—slack moment. A good many of the young chaps come in for Vegenin or aspirin when they've got a hangover—and occasionally, I'd say, for a flirtatious word or two with one of the girls if the opportunity arises. Human nature is always human nature. You see how it is. Pretty hopeless.'

Poirot said, 'And if I recollect rightly, one or more of the students at Hickory Road is attached to St Catherine's—a big red-haired boy—Bates—Bateman—'

'Leonard Bateson. That's right. And Colin McNabb is doing a post-graduate course there. Then there's a girl, Jean Tomlinson, who works in the physiotherapy department.'

'And all of these have probably been quite often in the Dispensary?'

'Yes, and what's more, nobody remembers when because they're used to seeing them and know them by sight. Jean Tomlinson was by way of being a friend of the senior dispenser—'

'It is not easy,' said Poirot.

'I'll say it's not! You see, anyone who was on the staff could take a look in the poison cupboard, and say, "Why on earth do you have so much Liquor Arsenicalis?" or something like that. "Didn't know anybody used it nowadays." And nobody would think twice about it or remember it.'

Sharpe paused and then said:

'What we are postulating is that someone gave Celia Austin morphia and afterwards put the morphia bottle and the torn-out fragment of letter in her room to make it look like suicide. But why, M. Poirot, why?'

Poirot shook his head. Sharpe went on:

'You hinted this morning that someone might have suggested the kleptomania idea to Celia Austin.'

Poirot moved uneasily.

'That was only a vague idea of mine. It was just that it

seemed doubtful if she would have had the wits to think of it herself.'

'Then who?'

'As far as I know, only three of the students would have been capable of thinking out such an idea. Leonard Bateson would have had the requisite knowledge. He is aware of Colin's enthusiasm for "maladjusted personalities." He might have suggested something of the kind to Celia more or less as a joke and coached her in her part. But I cannot really see him conniving at such a thing for month after month—unless, that is, he had an ulterior motive, or is a very different person from what he appears to be. (That is always a thing one must take into account.) Nigel Chapman has a mischievous and slightly malicious turn of mind. He'd think it good fun, and I should imagine would have no scruples whatever. He is a kind of grown up "*enfant terrible*." The third person I have in mind is a young woman called Valerie Hobhouse. She has brains, is modern in outlook and education, and has probably read enough psychology to judge Colin's probable reaction. If she were fond of Celia, she might think it legitimate fun to make a fool of Colin.'

'Leonard Bateson, Nigel Chapman, Valerie Hobhouse,' said Sharpe, writing down the names. 'Thanks for the tip. I'll remember when I'm questioning them. What about the Indians? One of them is a medical student.'

'His mind is entirely occupied with politics and persecution mania,' said Poirot. 'I don't think he would be interested enough to suggest kleptomania to Celia Austin and I don't think she would have accepted such advice from him.'

'And that's all the help you can give me, M. Poirot?' said Sharpe, rising to his feet and buttoning away his notebook.

'I fear so. But I consider myself personally interested—that is if you do not object, my friend?'

'Not in the least. Why should I?'

'In my own amateurish way I shall do what I can. For me, there is, I think, only one line of action.'

'And that is?'

Poirot sighed.

'*Conversation*, my friend. Conversation and again conversation! All the murderers I have ever come across enjoyed talking. In my opinion the strong silent man seldom commits a crime—and if he does it is simple, violent, and perfectly obvious. But our clever subtle murderer—he is so pleased with himself that sooner or later he says something unfortunate and trips himself up. Talk to these people, *mon cher*, do not confine yourself to simple interrogation. Encourage their views, demand their help, inquire about their hunches—but, *bon dieu*! I do not need to teach you your business. I remember your abilities well enough.'

Sharpe smiled gently.

'Yes,' he said, 'I've always found—well—amiability—a great help.'

The two men smiled at each other in mutual accord.

Sharpe rose to depart.

'I suppose every single one of them is a possible murderer,' he said slowly.

'I should think so,' said Poirot nonchalantly. 'Leonard Bateson, for instance, has a temper. He could lose control. Valerie Hobhouse has brains and could plan cleverly. Nigel Chapman is the childish type that lacks proportion. There is a French girl there who might kill if enough money were involved. Patricia Lane is a maternal type and maternal types are always ruthless. The American girl, Sally Finch, is cheerful and gay, but she could play an assumed part better than most. Jean Tomlinson is very full of sweetness and righteousness but we have all known killers who attended Sunday school with sincere devotion. The West Indian girl Elizabeth Johnston has probably the best brains of anyone in the hostel. She has subordinated her emotional life to her brain—that is dangerous. There is a charming young African who might have motives for killing about which we could never guess. We have Colin McNabb, the psychologist. How many psychologists does one know to whom it might be said *Physician, heal thyself*?'

'For heaven's sake, Poirot. You are making my head spin! Is nobody incapable of murder?'

'I have often wondered,' said Hercule Poirot.

CHAPTER NINE

Inspector Sharpe sighed, leaned back in his chair and rubbed his forehead with a handkerchief. He had interviewed an indignant and tearful French girl, a supercilious and unco-operative young Frenchman, a stolid and suspicious Dutchman, a voluble and aggressive Egyptian. He had exchanged a few brief remarks with two nervous young Turkish students who did not really understand what he was saying and the same went for a charming young Iraqi. None of these, he was pretty certain, had had anything to do, or could help him in any way with the death of Celia Austin. He had dismissed them one by one with a few reassuring words and was now preparing to do the same to Mr Akibombo.

The young West African looked at him with smiling white teeth and rather childlike, plaintive, eyes.

'I should like to help—yes—please,' he said. 'She is very nice to me, this Miss Celia. She give me once a box of Edinburgh rock—very nice confection which I do not know before. It seems very sad she should be killed. Is it blood feud, perhaps? Or is it perhaps fathers or uncles who come and kill her because they have heard false stories that she do wrong things.'

Inspector Sharpe assured him that none of these things were remotely possible. The young man shook his head sadly.

'Then I do not know why it happened,' he said. 'I do not see why anybody here should want to do harm to her. But you give me piece of her hair and nail clippings,' he continued, 'and I see if I find out by old method. Not scientific, not modern, but very much in use where I come from.'

'Well, thank you, Mr Akibombo, but I don't think that will be necessary. We—er—don't do things that way over here.'

'No, sir, I quite understand. Not modern. Not atomic age. Not done at home now by new policemen—only old men from bush. I am sure all new methods very superior and sure to achieve complete success.' Mr Akibombo bowed politely and removed himself. Inspector Sharpe murmured to himself:

'I sincerely hope we do meet with success—if only to maintain prestige.'

His next interview was with Nigel Chapman, who was inclined to take the conduct of the conversation into his own hands.

'This is an absolutely extraordinary business, isn't it?' he said. 'Mind you, I had an idea that you were barking up the wrong tree when you insisted on suicide. I must say, it's rather gratifying to me to think that the whole thing hinges, really, on her having filled her fountain-pen with my green ink. Just the one thing the murderer couldn't possibly foresee. I suppose you've given due consideration as to what can possibly be the motive for this crime?'

'I'm asking the questions, Mr Chapman,' said Inspector Sharpe dryly.

'Oh, of course, of course,' said Nigel, airily, waving a hand. 'I was trying to make a bit of a short-cut of it, that was all. But I suppose we've got to go through with all the red tape as usual. Name, Nigel Chapman. Age, twenty-five. Born, I believe, in Nagasaki—it really seems a most ridiculous place. What my father and mother were doing there at the time I can't imagine. On a world tour, I suppose. However, it doesn't make me necessarily a Japanese, I understand. I'm taking a diploma at London University in Bronze Age and Medieval History. Anything else you want to know?'

'What is your home address, Mr Chapman?'

'No home address, my dear sir. I have a papa, but he and I have quarrelled, and his address is therefore no longer mine. So 26 Hickory Road and Coutts Bank, Leadenhall Street Branch, will always find me, as one says to travelling acquaintances whom you hope you will never meet again.'

Inspector Sharpe displayed no reaction towards Nigel's

airy impertinence. He had met Nigels before and shrewdly suspected that Nigel's impertinence masked a natural nervousness of being questioned in connection with murder.

'How well did you know Celia Austin?' he asked.

'That's really quite a difficult question. I knew her very well in the sense of seeing her practically every day, and being on quite cheerful terms with her, but actually I didn't *know* her at all. Of course, I wasn't in the least bit interested in her and I think she probably disapproved of me, if anything.'

'Did she disapprove of you for any particular reason?'

'Well, she didn't like my sense of humour very much. Then, of course, I wasn't one of those brooding, rude young men like Colin McNabb. That kind of rudeness is really the perfect technique for attracting women.'

'When was the last time you saw Celia Austin?'

'At dinner yesterday evening. We'd all given her the big hand, you know. Colin had got up and hemmed and hawed and finally admitted, in a coy and bashful way, that they were engaged. Then we all ragged him a bit, and that was that.'

'Was that at dinner or in the common-room?'

'Oh, at dinner. Afterwards, when we went into the common-room Colin went off somewhere.'

'And the rest of you had coffee in the common-room.'

'If you call the fluid they serve coffee—yes,' said Nigel.

'Did Celia Austin have coffee?'

'Well, I suppose so. I mean, I didn't actually notice her having coffee, but she must have had it.'

'You did not personally hand her her coffee, for instance?'

'How horribly suggestive all this is! When you said that and looked at me in that searching way, d'you know I felt quite certain that I had handed Celia her coffee and had filled it up with strychnine, or whatever it was. Hypnotic suggestion, I suppose, but actually, Mr Sharpe, I didn't go near her—and to be frank, I didn't even notice her drinking coffee, and I can assure you, whether you believe me or not, that I have never had any passion for Celia myself and that the announcement of her engagement to Colin McNabb aroused no feelings of murderous revenge in me.'

'I'm not really suggesting anything of the kind, Mr Chapman,' said Sharpe mildly. 'Unless I'm very much mistaken, there's no particular love angle to this, but somebody wanted Celia Austin out of the way. Why?'

'I simply can't imagine why, Inspector. It's really most intriguing because Celia was really a most harmless kind of girl, if you know what I mean. Slow on the uptake; a bit of a bore; thoroughly nice; and absolutely, I should say, not the kind of girl to get herself murdered.'

'Were you surprised when you found that it was Celia Austin who had been responsible for the various disappearances, thefts, etcetera, in this place?'

'My dear man, you could have knocked me over with a feather! Most uncharacteristic, that's what I thought.'

'You didn't, perhaps, put her up to doing these things?'

Nigel's stare of surprise seemed quite genuine.

'I? Put her up to it? Why should I?'

'Well, that would be rather the question, wouldn't it? Some people have a funny sense of humour.'

'Well, really, I may be dense, but I can't see anything amusing about all this silly pilfering that's been going on.'

'Not your idea of a joke?'

'It never occurred to me it was meant to be funny. Surely, Inspector, the thefts were purely psychological?'

'You definitely consider that Celia Austin was a kleptomaniac?'

'But surely there can't be any other explanation, Inspector?'

'Perhaps you don't know as much about kleptomaniacs as I do, Mr Chapman.'

'Well, I really can't think of any other explanation.'

'You don't think it's possible that someone might have put Miss Austin up to all this as a means of—say—arousing Mr McNabb's interest in her?'

Nigel's eyes glistened with appreciative malice.

'Now that really is a most diverting explanation, Inspector,' he said. 'You know, when I think of it, it's perfectly possible and of course old Colin would swallow it, line, hook and sinker.' Nigel savoured this with much glee for a second or two. Then he shook his head sadly.

'But Celia wouldn't have played,' he said. 'She was a serious girl. She'd never have made fun of Colin. She was soppy about him.'

'You've no theory of your own, Mr Chapman, about the things that have been going on in this house? About, for instance, the spilling of ink over Miss Johnston's papers?'

'If you're thinking I did it, Inspector Sharpe, that's quite untrue. Of course, it looks like me because of the green ink, but if you ask *me*, that was just spite.'

'What was spite?'

'Using my ink. Somebody deliberately used my ink to make it look like me. There's a lot of spite about here, Inspector.'

The inspector looked at him sharply.

'Now what exactly do you mean by a lot of spite about?'

But Nigel immediately drew back into his shell and became noncommittal.

'I didn't mean anything really—just that when a lot of people are cooped up together, they get rather petty.'

The next person on Inspector Sharpe's list was Leonard Bateson. Len Bateson was even less at his ease than Nigel, though it showed in a different way. He was suspicious and truculent.

'All right!' he burst out, after the first routine inquiries were concluded. '*I* poured out Celia's coffee and gave it to her. So what?'

'You gave her her after-dinner coffee—is that what you're saying, Mr Bateson?'

'Yes. At least I filled the cup up from the urn and put it down beside her and you can believe it or not, but there was no morphia in it.'

'You saw her drink it?'

'No, I didn't actually see her drink it. We were all moving around and I got into an argument with someone just after that. I didn't notice when she drank it. There were other people round her.'

'I see. In fact, what you are saying is that *anybody* could have dropped morphia into her coffee cup?'

'You try and put anything in anyone's cup! Everybody would see you.'

'Not necessarily,' said Sharpe.

Len burst out aggressively:

'What the hell do you think I want to poison the kid for? I'd nothing against her.'

'I've not suggested that you did want to poison her.'

'She took the stuff herself. She must have taken it herself. There's no other explanation.'

'We might think so, if it weren't for that faked suicide note.'

'Faked my hat! She wrote it, didn't she?'

'She wrote it as part of a letter, early that morning.'

'Well—she could have torn a bit out and used it as a suicide note.'

'Come now, Mr Bateson. If you wanted to write a suicide note you'd write one. You wouldn't take a letter you'd written to somebody else and carefully tear out one particular phrase.'

'I might do. People do all sorts of funny things.'

'In that case, where is the rest of the letter?'

'How should I know? That's your business, not mine.'

'I'm making it my business. You'd be well advised, Mr Bateson, to answer my questions civilly.'

'Well, what do you want to know? I didn't kill the girl, and I'd no motive for killing her.'

'You liked her?'

Len said less aggressively:

'I liked her very much. She was a nice kid. A bit dumb, but nice.'

'You believed her when she owned up to having committed the thefts which had been worrying everyone for some time past?'

'Well, I believed her, of course, since she said so. But I must say it seemed odd.'

'You didn't think it was a likely thing for her to do?'

'Well, no. Not really.'

Leonard's truculence had subsided now that he was no longer on the defensive and was giving his mind to a problem which obviously intrigued him.

'She didn't seem to be the type of a kleptomaniac, if you know what I mean,' he said. 'Nor a thief either.'

'And you can't think of any other reason for her having done what she did?'

'Other reason? What other reason could there be?'

'Well, she might have wanted to arouse the interest of Mr Colin McNabb.'

'That's a bit far-fetched, isn't it?'

'But it did arouse his interest.'

'Yes, of course it did. Old Colin's absolutely dead keen on any kind of psychological abnormality.'

'Well, then. If Celia Austin knew that . . .'

Len shook his head.

'You're wrong there. She wouldn't have been capable of thinking a thing like that out. Of planning it, I mean. She hadn't got the knowledge.'

'You've got the knowledge, though, haven't you?'

'What do you mean?'

'I mean that, out of a purely kindly intention, you might have suggested something of the kind to her.'

Len gave a short laugh.

'Think I'd do a damfool thing like that? You're crazy.'

The inspector shifted his ground.

'Do you think that Celia Austin spilled the ink over Elizabeth Johnston's papers or do you think someone else did it?'

'Someone else. Celia said she didn't do that and I believe her. Celia never got riled by Bess; not like some other people did.'

'Who got riled by her—and why?'

'She ticked people off, you know.' Len thought about it for a moment or two. 'Anyone who made a rash statement. She'd look across the table and she'd say, in that precise way of hers, "I'm afraid that is not borne out by the facts. It has been well established by statistics that . . ." Something of that kind. Well, it was riling, you know—especially to people who like making rash statements, like Nigel Chapman for instance.'

'Ah yes. Nigel Chapman.'

'And it was green ink, too.'

'So you think it was Nigel who did it?'

'Well, it's possible, at least. He's a spiteful sort of cove, you know, and I think he might have a bit of racial feeling. About the only one of us who has.'

'Can you think of anybody else who Miss Johnston annoyed with her exactitude and her habit of correction?'

'Well, Colin McNabb wasn't too pleased, now and again, and she got Jean Tomlinson's goat once or twice.'

Sharpe asked a few more desultory questions but Len Bateson had nothing useful to add. Next Sharpe saw Valerie Hobhouse.

Valerie was cool, elegant, and wary. She displayed much less nervousness than either of the men had done. She had been fond of Celia, she said. Celia was not particularly bright and it was rather pathetic the way she had set her heart on Colin McNabb.

'Do you think she was a kleptomaniac, Miss Hobhouse?'

'Well, I suppose so. I don't really know much about the subject.'

'Do you think anyone had put her up to doing what she did?'

Valerie shrugged her shoulders.

'You mean in order to attract that pompous ass Colin?'

'You're very quick on the point, Miss Hobhouse. Yes, that's what I mean. You didn't suggest it to her yourself, I suppose?'

Valerie looked amused.

'Well, hardly, my dear man, considering that a particularly favourite scarf of mine was cut to ribbons. I'm not so altruistic as that.'

'Do you think anybody else suggested it to her?'

'I should hardly think so. I should say it was just natural on her part.'

'What do you mean by natural?'

'Well, I first had a suspicion that it was Celia when all

the fuss happened about Sally's shoe. Celia was jealous of Sally. Sally Finch, I'm talking about. She's far and away the most attractive girl here and Colin paid her a fair amount of attention. So on the night of this party Sally's shoe disappears and she has to go in an old black dress and black shoes. There was Celia looking as smug as a cat that's swallowed cream about it. Mind you, I didn't suspect her of all these petty thievings of bracelets and compacts.'

'Who did you think was responsible for those?'

Valerie shrugged her shoulders.

'Oh, I don't know. One of the cleaning women, I thought.'

'And the slashed rucksack?'

'Was there a slashed rucksack? I'd forgotten. That seems very pointless.'

'You've been here a good long time, haven't you, Miss Hobhouse?'

'Well, yes. I should say I'm probably the oldest inhabitant. That is to say, I've been here two years and a half now.'

'So you probably know more about this hostel than anybody else?'

'I should say so, yes.'

'Have you any ideas of your own about Celia Austin's death? Any idea of the motive that underlay it?'

Valerie shook her head. Her face was serious now.

'No,' she said. 'It was a horrible thing to happen. I can't see anybody who could possibly have wanted Celia to die. She was a nice, harmless child, and she'd just got engaged to be married, and . . .'

'Yes. And?' the Inspector prompted.

'I wondered if that was why,' said Valerie slowly. 'Because she'd got engaged. Because she was going to be happy. But that means, doesn't it, somebody—well—mad.'

She said the word with a little shiver, and Inspector Sharpe looked at her thoughtfully.

'Yes,' he said. 'We can't quite rule out madness.' He went on, 'Have you any theory about the damage done to Elizabeth Johnston's notes and papers?'

'No. That was a spiteful thing, too. I don't believe for a

moment that Celia would do a thing like that.'

'Any idea who it could have been?'

'Well . . . Not a reasonable idea.'

'But an unreasonable one?'

'You don't want to hear something that's just a hunch, do you, Inspector?'

'I'd like to hear a hunch very much. I'll accept it as such, and it'll only be between ourselves.'

'Well, I may probably be quite wrong, but I've got a sort of idea that it was Patricia Lane's work.'

'Indeed! Now you do surprise me, Miss Hobhouse. I shouldn't have thought of Patricia Lane. She seems a very well balanced, amiable, young lady.'

'I don't say she did do it. I just had a sort of idea she might have done.'

'For what reason in particular?'

'Well, Patricia disliked Black Bess. Black Bess was always ticking off Patricia's beloved Nigel, putting him right, you know, when he made silly statements in the way he does sometimes.'

'You think it was more likely to have been Patricia Lane than Nigel himself?'

'Oh, yes. I don't think Nigel would bother, and he'd certainly not go using his own pet brand of ink. He's got plenty of brains. But it's just the sort of stupid thing that Patricia would do without thinking that it might involve her precious Nigel as a suspect.'

'Or again, it might be somebody who had a down on Nigel Chapman and wanted to suggest that it was his doing?'

'Yes, that's another possibility.'

'Who dislikes Nigel Chapman?'

'Oh, well, Jean Tomlinson for one. And he and Len Bateson are always scrapping a good deal.'

'Have you any ideas, Miss Hobhouse, how morphia could have been administered to Celia Austin?'

'I've been thinking and thinking. Of course, I suppose the coffee is the most obvious way. We were all milling around in the common-room. Celia's coffee was on a small table near her and she always waited until her coffee was nearly cold before she drank it. I suppose anybody who had sufficient nerve could have dropped a tablet or something into her cup without being seen, but it would be rather a risk to take. I mean, it's the sort of thing that might be noticed quite easily.'

'The morphia,' said Inspector Sharpe, 'was not in tablet form.'

'What was it? Powder?'

'Yes.'

Valerie frowned.

'That would be rather more difficult, wouldn't it?'

'Anything else besides coffee you can think of?'

'She sometimes had a glass of hot milk before she went to bed. I don't think she did that night, though.'

'Can you describe to me exactly what happened that evening in the common-room?'

'Well, as I say, we all sat about, talked; somebody turned the wireless on. Most of the boys, I think, went out. Celia went up to bed fairly early and so did Jean Tomlinson. Sally and I sat on there fairly late. I was writing letters and Sally was mugging over some notes. I rather think I was the last to go up to bed.'

'It was just a usual evening, in fact?'

'Absolutely, Inspector.'

'Thank you, Miss Hobhouse. Will you send Miss Lane to me now?'

Patricia Lane looked worried, but not apprehensive. Questions and answers elicited nothing very new. Asked about the damage to Elizabeth Johnston's papers Patricia said that she had no doubt that Celia had been responsible.

'But she denied it, Miss Lane, very vehemently.'

'Well, of course,' said Patricia. 'She would. I think she was ashamed of having done it. But it fits in, doesn't it, with all the other things?'

'Do you know what I find about this case, Miss Lane? That nothing fits in very well.'

'I suppose,' said Patricia, flushing, 'that you think it was Nigel who messed up Bess's papers. Because of the ink.

That's such absolute *nonsense*. I mean, Nigel wouldn't have used his own ink if he'd done a thing like that. He wouldn't be such a fool. But anyway, he wouldn't do it.'

'He didn't always get on very well with Miss Johnston, did he?'

'Oh, she had an annoying manner sometimes, but he didn't really mind.' Patricia Lane leaned forward earnestly. 'I would like to try and make you understand one or two things, Inspector. About Nigel Chapman, I mean. You see, Nigel is really very much his own worst enemy. I'm the first to admit that he's got a very difficult manner. It prejudices people against him. He's rude and sarcastic and makes fun of people, and so he puts people's backs up and they think the worst of him. But really he's quite different from what he seems. He's one of those shy, rather unhappy people who really want to be liked but who, from a kind of spirit of contradiction, find themselves saying and doing the opposite to what they mean to say and do.'

'Ah,' said Inspector Sharpe. 'Rather unfortunate for them, that.'

'Yes, but they really can't help it, you know. It comes from having had an unfortunate chlidhood. Nigel had a very unhappy home life. His father was very harsh and severe and never understood him. And his father treated his mother very badly. After she died they had the most terrific quarrel and Nigel flung out of the house, and his father said that he'd never give him a penny and he must get on as well as he could without any help from him. Nigel said he didn't want any help from his father; and wouldn't take it if it was offered. A small amount of money came to him under his mother's will, and he never wrote to his father or went near him again. Of course, I think that was a pity in a way, but there's no doubt that his father is a very unpleasant man. I don't wonder that that's made Nigel bitter and difficult to get on with. Since his mother died, he's never had anyone to care for him and look after him. His health's not been good, though his mind is brilliant. He is handicapped in life and he just can't show himself as he really is.'

Patricia Lane stopped. She was flushed and a little breathless as the result of her long earnest speech. Inspector Sharpe looked at her thoughtfully. He had come across many Patricia Lanes before. 'In love with the chap,' he thought to himself. 'Don't suppose he cares twopence for her, but probably accepted being mothered. Father certainly sounds a cantankerous old cuss, but I dare say the mother was a foolish woman who spoilt her son and by doting on him, widened the breach between him and his father. I've seen enough of that kind of thing.' He wondered if Nigel Chapman had been attracted at all to Celia Austin. It seemed unlikely, but it might be so. 'And if so,' he thought, 'Patricia Lane might have bitterly resented the fact.' Resented it enough to wish to do Celia an injury? Resented it enough to do murder? Surely not—and in any case, the fact that Celia had got engaged to Colin McNabb would surely wash that out as a possible motive for murder. He dismissed Patricia Lane and asked for Jean Tomlinson.

CHAPTER TEN

Miss Tomlinson was a severe-looking young woman of twenty-seven, with fair hair, regular features and a rather pursed-up mouth. She sat down and said primly:

'Yes, Inspector? What can I do for you?'

'I wonder if you can help us at all, Miss Tomlinson, about this very tragic matter.'

'It's shocking. Really quite shocking,' said Jean. 'It was bad enough when we thought Celia had committed suicide, but now that it's supposed to be murder . . .' She stopped and shook her head, sadly.

'We are fairly sure that she did not poison herself,' said Sharpe. 'You know where the poison came from?'

Jean nodded.

'I gather it came from St Catherine's Hospital, where she works. But surely that makes it seem more like suicide?'

'It was intended to, no doubt,' said the inspector.

'But who else could possibly have got that poison except Celia?'

'Quite a lot of people,' said Inspector Sharpe, 'if they were determined to do so. Even you, yourself, Miss Tomlinson,' he said, 'might have managed to help yourself to it if you had wished to do so.'

'Really, Inspector Sharpe!' Jean's tones were sharp with indignation.

'Well, you visited the Dispensary fairly often, didn't you, Miss Tomlinson?'

'I went in there to see Mildred Carey, yes. But naturally I would never have dreamed of tampering with the poison cupboard.'

'But you could have done so?'

'I certainly couldn't have done anything of the kind!'

'Oh, come now, Miss Tomlinson. Say that your friend was busy packing up the ward baskets and the other girl was at the outpatients' window. There are frequent times when there are only two dispensers in the front room. You could have wandered casually round the back of the shelves of bottles that run across the middle of the floor. You could have nipped a bottle out of the cupboard and into your pocket, and neither of the two dispensers would have dreamed of what you had done.'

'I resent what you say very much, Inspector Sharpe. It's —it's a—disgraceful accusation.'

'But it's not an accusation, Miss Tomlinson. It's nothing of the kind. You mustn't misunderstand me. You said to me that it wasn't possible for you to do such a thing, and I'm trying to show you that it was *possible*. I'm not suggesting for a moment that you did do so. After all,' he added, 'why should you?'

'Quite so. You don't seem to realise, Inspector Sharpe, that I was a friend of Celia's.'

'Quite a lot of people get poisoned by their friends. There's a certain question we have to ask ourselves sometimes. "When is a friend not a friend?"'

'There was no disagreement between me and Celia; nothing of the kind. I liked her very much.'

'Had you any reason to suspect it was she who had been responsible for these thefts in the house?'

'No, indeed. I was never so surprised in my life. I always thought Celia had high principles. I wouldn't have dreamed of her doing such a thing.'

'Of course,' said Sharpe, watching her carefully, 'kleptomaniacs can't really help themselves, can they?'

Jean Tomlinson's lips pursed themselves together even more closely. Then she opened them and spoke.

'I can't say I can quite subscribe to *that* idea, Inspector Sharpe. I'm old-fashioned in my views and believe that stealing is stealing.'

'You think that Celia stole things because, frankly, she wanted to take them?'

'Certainly I do.'

'Plain dishonest, in fact?'

'I'm afraid so.'

'Ah!' said Inspector Sharpe, shaking his head. 'That's bad.'

'Yes, it's always upsetting when you feel you're disappointed in anyone.'

'There was a question, I understand, of our being called in—the police, I mean.'

'Yes. That would have been the right thing to do in my opinion.'

'Perhaps you think it ought to have been done anyway?'

'I think it would have been the right thing. Yes, I don't think, you know, people ought to be allowed to get away with these things.'

'With calling oneself a kleptomaniac when one is really a thief, do you mean?'

'Well, more or less, yes—that is what I mean.'

'Instead of which everything was ending happily and Miss Austin had wedding bells ahead.'

'Of course, one isn't surprised at anything Colin McNabb does,' said Jean Tomlinson viciously. 'I'm sure he's an atheist and a most disbelieving, mocking, unpleasant young man. He's rude to everybody. It's my opinion that he's a *Communist*!'

'Ah!' said Inspector Sharpe. 'Bad!' He shook his head.

'He backed up Celia, I think, because he hasn't got any proper feeling about property. He probably thinks everyone should help themselves to everything they want.'

'Still, at any rate,' said Inspector Sharpe, 'Miss Austin did own up.'

'After she was found out. Yes,' said Jean sharply.

'Who found her out?'

'That Mr—what-was-his-name . . . Poirot, who came.'

'But why do you think he found her out, Miss Tomlinson? He didn't say so. He just advised calling in the police.'

'He must have shown her that he knew. She obviously knew the game was up and rushed off to confess.'

'What about the ink on Elizabeth Johnston's papers? Did she confess to that?'

'I really don't know. I suppose so.'

'You suppose wrong,' said Sharpe. 'She denied most

vehemently that she had anything to do with that.'

'Well, perhaps that may be so. I must say it doesn't seem very likely.'

'You think it is more likely that it was Nigel Chapman?'

'No, I don't think Nigel would do that either. I think it's much more likely to be Mr Akibombo.'

'Really? Why should he do it?'

'Jealousy. All these coloured people are very jealous of each other and very hysterical.'

'That's interesting, Miss Tomlinson. When was the last time you saw Celia Austin?'

'After dinner on Friday night.'

'Who went up to bed first? Did she or did you?'

'I did.'

'You did not go to her room or see her after you'd left the common-room?'

'No.'

'And you've no idea who could have introduced morphia into her coffee—if it was given that way?'

'No idea at all.'

'You never saw this morphia lying about the house or in anyone's room?'

'No. No, I don't think so.'

'You don't think so? What do you mean by that, Miss Tomlinson?'

'Well, I just wondered. There was that silly bet, you know.'

'What bet?'

'One—oh, two or three of the boys were arguing—'

'What were they arguing about?'

'Murder, and ways of doing it. Poisoning in particular.'

'Who was concerned in the discussion?'

'Well, I think Colin and Nigel started it, and then Len Bateson chipped in and Patricia was there too—'

'Can you remember, as closely as possible, what was said on that occasion—how the argument went?'

Jean Tomlinson reflected a few moments.

'Well, it started, I think, with a discussion on murdering

by poisoning, saying that the difficulty was to get hold of the poison, that the murderer was usually traced by either the sale of the poison or having an opportunity to get it, and Nigel said that wasn't at all necessary. He said that he could think of three distinct ways by which anyone could get hold of poison, and nobody would ever know they had it. Len Bateson said then that he was talking through his hat. Nigel said no he wasn't, and he was quite prepared to prove it. Pat said that of course Nigel was quite right. She said that either Len or Colin could probably help themselves to poison any time they liked from a hospital, and so could Celia, she said. And Nigel said that wasn't what he meant at all. He said it would be noticed if Celia took anything from the Dispensary. Sooner or later they'd look for it and find it gone. And Pat said no, not if she took the bottle and emptied some stuff out and filled it up with something else. Colin laughed then and said there'd be very serious complaints from the patients one of these days, in that case. But Nigel said of course he didn't mean special opportunities. He said that he himself, who hadn't got any particular access, either as a doctor or dispenser, could jolly well get three different kinds of poison by three different methods. Len Bateson said, "All right, then, but what are your methods?" and Nigel said, "I shan't tell you, now, but I'm prepared to bet you that within three weeks I can produce samples of three deadly poisons here," and Len Bateson said he'd bet him a fiver he couldn't do it.'

'Well?' said Inspector Sharpe, when Jean stopped.

'Well, nothing more came of it, I think, for some time and then, one evening, in the common-room, Nigel said, "Now then, chaps, look here—I'm as good as my word," and he threw down three things on the table. He had a tube of hyoscine tablets, and a bottle of tincture of digitalin, and a tiny bottle of morphine tartrate.'

The inspector said sharply:

'Morphine tartrate. Any label on it.'

'Yes, it had St Catherine's Hospital on it. I do remember that because, naturally, it caught my eye.'

'And the others?'

'I didn't notice. They were not hospital stores, I should say.'

'What happened next?'

'Well, of course, there was a lot of talk and jawing, and Len Bateson said, "Come now, if you'd done a murder this would be traced to you soon enough," and Nigel said, "Not a bit of it. I'm a layman. I've no connection with any clinic or hospital and nobody will connect me for one moment with these. I didn't buy them over the counter," and Colin McNabb took his pipe out of his teeth and said, "No, you'd certainly not be able to do that. There's no chemist would sell you those three things without a doctor's prescription." Anyway, they argued a bit but in the end Len said he'd pay up. He said, "I can't do it now, because I'm a bit short of cash, but there's no doubt about it; Nigel's proved his point," and then he said, "What are we going to do with the guilty spoils?" Nigel grinned and said we'd better get rid of them before any accidents occurred, so they emptied out the tube and threw the tablets on the fire and emptied out the powder from the morphine tartrate and threw that on the fire too. The tincture of digitalis they poured down the lavatory.'

'And the bottles?'

'I don't know what happened to the bottles . . . I should think they probably were just thrown into the waste-paper basket?'

'But the poison itself was destroyed?'

'Yes. I'm sure of that. I saw it.'

'And that was—when?'

'About, oh, just over a fortnight ago, I think.'

'I see. Thank you, Miss Tomlinson.'

Jean lingered, clearly wanting to be told more.

'D'you think it might be important?'

'It might be. One can't tell.'

Inspector Sharpe remained brooding for a few moments. Then he had Nigel Chapman in again.

'I've just had a rather interesting statement from Miss Jean Tomlinson,' he said.

'Ah! Who's dear Jean been poisoning your mind against? Me?'

'She's been talking about poison, and in connection with you, Mr Chapman.'

'Poison and me? What on earth?'

'Do you deny that some weeks ago you had a wager with Mr Bateson about methods of obtaining poison in some way that could not be traced to you?'

'Oh that!' Nigel was suddenly enlightened. 'Yes, of course! Funny I never thought of that. I don't even remember Jean being there. But you don't think it could have any possible significance, do you?'

'Well, one doesn't know. You admit the fact, then?'

'Oh yes, we were arguing on the subject. Colin and Len were being very superior and high-handed about it so I told them that with a little ingenuity anyone could get hold of a suitable supply of poison—in fact I said I could think of three distinct ways of doing it, and I'd prove my point, I said, by putting them into practice.'

'Which you then proceeded to do?'

'Which I then proceeded to do, Inspector.'

'And what were those three methods, Mr Chapman?'

Nigel put his head a little on one side.

'Aren't you asking me to incriminate myself?' he said. 'Surely you ought to warn me?'

'It hasn't come to warning you yet, Mr Chapman, but, of course, there's no need for you to incriminate yourself, as you put it. In fact you're perfectly entitled to refuse my questions if you like to do so.'

'I don't know that I want to refuse.' Nigel considered for a moment or two, a slight smile playing round his lips.

'Of couse,' he said, 'what I did was, no doubt, against the law. You could haul me in for it if you liked. On the other hand, this is a murder case and if it's got any bearing on poor little Celia's death I suppose I ought to tell you.'

'That would certainly be the sensible point of view to take.'

'All right then. I'll talk.'

'What were these three methods?'

'Well.' Nigel leant back in his chair. 'One's always reading in the papers, isn't one, about doctors losing dangerous drugs from a car? People are being warned about it.'

'Yes.'

'Well, it occurred to me that one very simple method, would be to go down to the country, follow a G.P. about on his rounds, when occasion offered—just open the car, look in the doctor's case, and extract what you wanted. You see, in these country districts, the doctor doesn't always take his case into the house. It depends what sort of patient he's going to see.'

'Well?'

'Well, that's all. That's to say that's all for method number one. I had to sleuth three doctors until I had found a suitably careless one. When I did, it was simplicity itself. The car was left outside a farmhouse in a rather lonely spot. I opened the door, looked at the case, took out a tube of hyoscine hydrobromide, and that was that.'

'Ah! And method number two?'

'That entailed just a little pumping of dear Celia, as a matter of fact. She was quite unsuspicious. I told you she was a stupid girl, she had no idea what I was doing. I simply talked a bit about the mumbo jumbo Latin of doctors' prescriptions, and asked her to write me out a prescription in the way a doctor writes it, for tincture digitalis. She obliged quite unsuspecting. All I had to do after that was to find a doctor in the classified directory, living in a far off district of London, add his initials or slightly illegible signature. I then took it to a chemist in a busy part of London, who would not be likely to be familiar with that particular doctor's signature, and I received the prescription made up without any difficulty at all. Digitalin is prescribed in quite large quantities for heart cases and I had written out the prescription on hotel notepaper.'

'Very ingenious,' said Inspector Sharpe dryly.

'I *am* incriminating myself! I can hear it in your voice.'

'And the third method?'

Nigel did not reply at once. Then he said:

'Look here. What exactly am I letting myself in for?'

'The theft of drugs from an unlocked car is larceny,' said Inspector Sharpe. 'Forging a prescription . . .'

Nigel interrupted him.

'Not exactly forging, is it? I mean, I didn't obtain money by it, and it wasn't actually an imitation of any doctor's signature. I mean, if I write a prescription and write H. R. James, on it, you can't say I'm forging any particular Dr James's name, can you?' He went on with rather a wry smile. 'You see what I mean? I'm sticking my neck out. If you like to turn nasty over this—well—I'm obviously for it. On the other hand, if . . .'

'Yes, Mr Chapman, on the other hand?'

Nigel said with a sudden passion:

'I don't like murder. It's a beastly, horrible thing. Celia, poor little devil, didn't deserve to be murdered. I want to help. But does it help? I can't see that it does. Telling you my peccadilloes, I mean.'

'The police have a good deal of latitude, Mr Chapman. It's up to them to look upon certain happenings as a light-hearted prank of an irresponsible nature. I accept your assurance that you want to help in the solving of this girl's murder. Now please go on, and tell me about your third method.'

'Well,' said Nigel, 'we're coming fairly near the bone now. It was a bit more risky than the other two, but at the same time it was a great deal more fun. You see, I'd been to visit Celia once or twice in her Dispensary. I knew the lay of the land there . . .'

'So you were able to pinch the bottle out of the cupboard?'

'No, no, nothing as simple as that. That wouldn't have been fair from my point of view. And, incidentally, if it had been a *real* murder—that is, if I had been stealing the poison for the purpose of murder—it would probably be remembered that I had been there. Actually, I hadn't been in Celia's Dispensary for about six months. No, I knew Celia always went into the back room at eleven-fifteen for what you might call "elevenses," that is, a cup of coffee and a biscuit. The girls went in turn, two at a time. There was a new girl there who had only just come and she certainly wouldn't know me by sight. So what I did was this. I strolled into the Dispensary with a white coat on and a stethoscope round my neck. There was only the new girl there and she was busy at the outpatients' hatch. I strolled in, went along to the poison cupboard, took out a bottle, strolled round the end of the partition, said to the girl, "What strength adrenalin do you keep?" She told me and I nodded, then I asked her if she had a couple of Veganin as I had a terrific hangover. I swallowed them down and strolled out again. She never had the least suspicion that I wasn't somebody's houseman or a medical student. It was child's play. Celia never even knew I'd been there.'

'A stethoscope,' said Inspector Sharpe curiously. 'Where did you get a stethoscope?'

Nigel grinned suddenly.

'It was Len Bateson's,' he said. 'I pinched it.'

'From this house?'

'Yes.'

'So that explains the theft of the stethoscope. That was not Celia's doing.'

'Good lord no! Can't see a kleptomaniac stealing a stethoscope, can you?'

'What did you do with it afterwards?'

'Well, I had to pawn it,' said Nigel apologetically.

'Wasn't that a little hard on Bateson?'

'Very hard on him. But without explaining my methods, which I didn't mean to do, I couldn't tell him about it. However,' added Nigel cheerfully, 'I took him out not long after and gave him a hell of a party one evening.'

'You're a very irresponsible young man,' said Inspector Sharpe.

'You should have seen their faces,' said Nigel, his grin widening, 'when I threw down those three lethal preparations on the table and told them I had managed to pinch them without anybody being wise as to who took them.'

'What you're telling me is,' said the inspector, 'that you had three means of poisoning someone by three different poisons and that in each case the poison could not have been traced to you.'

Nigel nodded.

'That's fair enough,' he said. 'And given the circumstances it's not a very pleasant thing to admit. But the point is, that the poisons were all disposed of at least a fortnight ago or longer.'

'That is what you think, Mr Chapman, but it may not really be so.'

Nigel stared at him.

'What do you mean?'

'You had these things in your possession, how long?'

Nigel considered.

'Well, the tube of hyoscine about ten days, I suppose. The morphine tartrate, about four days. The tincture digitalin I'd only got that very afternoon.'

'And where did you keep these things—the hyoscine hydrobromide and the morphine tartrate, that is to say?'

'In the drawer of my chest-of-drawers, pushed to the back under my socks.'

'Did anyone know you had it there?'

'No. No, I'm sure they didn't.'

There had been, however, a faint hesitation in his voice which Inspector Sharpe noticed, but for the moment he did not press the point.

'Did you tell anyone what you were doing? Your methods? The way you were going about these things?'

'No. At least—no, I didn't.'

'You said "at least," Mr Chapman.'

'Well, I didn't actually. As a matter of fact, I was going to tell Pat, then I thought she wouldn't approve. She's very strict, Pat is, so I fobbed her off.'

'You didn't tell her about stealing the stuff from the doctor's car, or the prescription, or the morphia from the hospital?'

'Actually, I told her afterwards about the digitalin; that I'd written a prescription and got a bottle from the chemist, and about masquerading as a doctor at the hospital. I'm sorry to say Pat wasn't amused. I didn't tell her about pinching things from a car. I thought she'd go up in smoke.'

'Did you tell her you were going to destroy this stuff after you'd won the bet?'

'Yes. She was all worried and het up about it. Started to insist I took the things back or something like that.'

'That course of action never occurred to you yourself?'

'Good lord no! That would have been fatal; it would have landed me in no end of a row. No, we three just chucked the stuff on the fire and poured it down the loo and that was that. No harm done.'

'You say that, Mr Chapman, but it's quite possible that harm was done.'

'How can it have been, if the stuff was chucked away as I tell you?'·

'Has it ever occurred to you, Mr Chapman, that someone might have seen where you put those things, or found them perhaps, and that someone might have emptied morphia out of the bottle and replaced it with something else?'

'Good lord no!' Nigel stared at him. 'I never thought of anything of that kind. I don't believe it.'

'But it's a possibility, Mr Chapman.'

'But nobody could possibly have known.'

'I should say,' said the inspector dryly, 'that in a place of this kind a great deal more is known than you yourself might believe possible.'

'Snooping, you mean?'

'Yes.'

'Perhaps you're right there.'

'Which of the students might normally, at any time, be in your room?'

'Well, I share it with Len Bateson. Most of the men here have been in it now and again. Not the girls, of course. The girls aren't supposed to come to the bedroom floors on our side of the house. Propriety. Pure living.'

'They're not supposed to, but they might do so, I suppose?'

'Anyone *might*,' said Nigel. 'In the daytime. The afternoon, for instance, there's nobody about.'

'Does Miss Lane ever come to your room?'

'I hope you don't mean that the way it sounds, Inspector.

Pat comes to my room sometimes to replace some socks she's been darning. Nothing more than that.'

Leaning forward Inspector Sharpe said:

'You do realise, Mr Chapman, that the person who could most easily have taken some of that poison out of the bottle and substituted something else for it, was yourself?'

Nigel looked at him, his face suddenly hard and haggard.

'Yes,' he said. 'I've seen that just a minute and a half ago. I could have done just exactly that. But I'd no reason on earth for putting that girl out of the way, Inspector, and I didn't do it. Still, there it is—I quite realise that you've only got my word for it.'

CHAPTER ELEVEN

The story of the bet and the disposal of the poison was confirmed by Len Bateson and by Colin McNabb. Sharpe retained Colin McNabb after the others had gone.

'I don't want to cause you more pain than I can help, Mr McNabb,' he said. 'I can realise what it means to you for your fiancée to have been poisoned on the very night of your engagement.'

'There'll be no need to go into that aspect of it,' said Colin McNabb, his face immovable. 'You'll not need to concern yourself with my feelings. Just ask me any questions you like which you think may be useful to you.'

'It was your considered opinion that Celia Austin's behaviour had a psychological origin?'

'There's no doubt about it at all,' said Colin McNabb. 'If you'd like me to go into the theory of the thing . . .'

'No, no,' said Inspector Sharpe hastily. 'I'm taking your word for it as a student of psychology.'

'Her childhood had been particularly unfortunate. It had set up an emotional block. . . .'

'Quite so, quite so.' Inpector Sharpe was desperately anxious to avoid hearing the story of yet another unhappy childhood. Nigel's had been quite enough.

'You had been attracted to her for some time?'

'I would not say precisely that,' said Colin, considering the matter conscientiously. 'These things sometimes surprise you by the way they dawn upon you suddenly, like. Subconsciously no doubt, I had been attracted, but I was not aware of the fact. Since it was not my intention to marry young, I had no doubt set up a considerable resistance to the idea in my conscious mind.'

'Yes. Just so. Celia Austin was happy in her engagement to you? I mean, she expressed no doubts? Uncertainties? There was nothing she felt she ought to tell you?'

'She made a very full confession of all she'd been doing. There was nothing more in her mind to worry her.'

'And you were planning to get married—when?'

'Not for a considerable time. I'm not in a position at the moment to support a wife.'

'Had Celia any enemies here? Anyone who did not like her?'

'I can hardly believe so. I've given that point of view a great deal of thought, Inspector. Celia was well liked here. I'd say, myself, it was not a personal matter at all which brought about her end.'

'What do you mean by "not a personal matter"?'

'I do not wish to be very precise at the moment. It's only a vague kind of idea I have and I'm not clear about it myself.'

From that position the inspector could not budge him.

The last two students to be interviewed were Sally Finch and Elizabeth Johnston. The inspector took Sally Finch first.

Sally was an attractive girl with a mop of red hair and eyes that were bright and intelligent. After routine inquiries Sally Finch suddenly took the initiative.

'D'you know what I'd like to do, Inspector? I'd like to tell you just what I think. I personally. There's something all wrong about this house, something very wrong indeed. I'm sure of that.'

'You mean because Celia Austin was poisoned?'

'No, I mean before that. I've been feeling it for some time. I didn't like the things that were going on here. I didn't like that rucksack which was slashed about and I didn't like Valerie's scarf being cut to pieces. I didn't like Black Bess's notes being covered with ink. I was going to get out of here and get out quick. That's what I still mean to do; as soon, that is, as you let us go.'

'You mean you're afraid of something, Miss Finch?' Sally nodded her head.

'Yes. I'm afraid. There's something or someone here who's pretty ruthless. The whole place isn't—well, how shall I put it?—it isn't what it seems. No, no, Inspector, I don't mean Communists. I can see that just trembling on your lips. It's not Communists I mean. Perhaps it isn't even criminal. I don't know. But I'll bet you anything you like that awful old woman knows about it all.'

'What old woman? You don't mean Mrs Hubbard?'

'No. Not Ma Hubbard. She's a dear. I mean old Nicoletis. That old she-wolf.'

'That's interesting, Miss Finch. Can you be more definite? About Mrs Nicoletis, I mean.'

Sally shook her head.

'No. That's just what I can't be. All I can tell you is she gives me the creeps every time I pass her. Something queer is going on here, Inspector.'

'I wish you could be a little more definite.'

'So do I. You'll be thinking I'm fanciful. Well, perhaps I am, but other people feel it too. Akibombo does. He's scared. I believe Black Bess does, too, but she wouldn't let on. And I think, Inspector, that Celia knew something about it.'

'Knew something about what?'

'That's just it. What? But there were things she said. Said that last day. About clearing everything up. She had owned up to *her* part in what was going on, but she sort of hinted that there were other things she knew about and she wanted to get them cleared up too. I think she knew *something*, Inspector, about *someone*. That's the reason I think she was killed.'

'But if it was something as serious as that . . .'

Sally interrupted him.

'I'd say that she had no idea how serious it was. She wasn't bright, you know. She was pretty dumb. She'd got hold of something but she'd no idea that the something she'd got hold of was dangerous. Anyway, that's my hunch for what it's worth.'

'I see. Thank you. . . . Now the last time you saw Celia Austin was in the common-room after dinner last night, is that right?'

'That's right. At least, actually, I saw her after that.'

'You saw her after that? Where? In her room?'

'No. When I went up to bed she was going out of the front door just as I came out of the common-room.'

'Going out of the front door? Out of the house, do you mean?'

'Yes.'

'That's rather surprising. Nobody else has suggested that.'

'I dare say they didn't know. She certainly said good night and that she was going up to bed, and if I hadn't seen her I would have assumed that she *had* gone up to bed.'

'Whereas actually she went upstairs, put on some outdoor things and then left the house. Is that right?'

Sally nodded.

'And I think she was going out to meet someone.'

'I see. Someone from outside. Or could it have been one of the students?'

'Well, it's my hunch that it would be one of the students. You see, if she wanted to speak to somebody privately, there was nowhere very well she could do it in the house. Someone might have suggested that she should come out and meet them somewhere outside.'

'Have you any idea when she got in again?'

'No idea whatever.'

'Would Geronimo know, the manservant?'

'He'd know if she came in after eleven o'clock because that's the time he bolts and chains the door. Up to that time anyone can get in with their own key.'

'Do you know exactly what time it was when you saw her going out of the house?'

'I'd say it was about—ten. Perhaps a little past ten, but not much.'

'I see. Thank you, Miss Finch, for what you've told me.'

Last of all the inspector talked to Elizabeth Johnston. He was at once impressed with the quiet capability of the girl. She answered his questions with intelligent decision and then waited for him to proceed.

'Celia Austin,' he said, 'protested vehemently that it was not she who damaged your papers, Miss Johnston. Do you believe her?'

'I do not think Celia did that. No.'

'You don't know who did?'

'The obvious answer is Nigel Chapman. But it seems to me a little too obvious. Nigel is intelligent. He would not use his own ink.'

'And if not Nigel. Who then?'

'That is more difficult. But I think Celia knew who it was—or at least guessed.'

'Did she tell you so?'

'Not in so many words; but she came to my room on the evening of the day she died, before going down to dinner. She came to tell me that though she was responsible for the thefts she had not sabotaged my work. I told her that I accepted that assurance. I asked her if she knew who had done so?'

'And what did she say?'

'She said'—Elizabeth paused a moment, as though to be sure of the accuracy of what she was about to say—'she said, "I can't really be sure, because I don't see why. . . . It might have been a mistake or an accident . . . I'm sure whoever did it is very unhappy about it, and would really like to own up." Celia went on, "There are some things I don't understand, like the electric light bulbs the day the police came." '

Sharpe interrupted.

'What's this about the police and electric light bulbs?'

'I don't know. All Celia said was: "I didn't take them out." And then she said: "I wondered if it had anything to do with the passport?" I said, "What passport are you talking about?" And she said: "I think someone might have a forged passport." '

The inspector was silent for a moment or two.

Here at last some vague pattern seemed to be taking shape. A passport. . . .

He asked, 'What more did she say?'

'Nothing more. She just said: "Anyway I shall know more about it to-morrow." '

'She said that, did she? *I shall know more about it to-morrow.* That's a very significant remark, Miss Johnston.'

'Yes.'

The inspector was again silent as he reflected.

Something about a passport—and a visit from the police.
. . . Before coming to Hickory Road, he had carefully looked up the files. A fairly close eye was kept on hostels which housed foreign students. 26 Hickory Road had a good record. Such details as there were, were meagre and un-suggestive. A West African student wanted by the Sheffield police for living on a woman's earnings; the student in question had been at Hickory Road for a few days and had then gone elsewhere, and had in due course been gathered in and since deported. There had been a routine check of all hostels and boarding-houses for a Eurasian 'wanted to assist the police' in the murder of a publican's wife near Cam-bridge. That had been cleared up when the young man in question had walked into the police station at Hull and had given himself up for the crime. There had been an inquiry into a student's distribution of subversive pamphlets. All these occurrences had taken place some time ago and could not possibly have any connection with the death of Celia Austin.

He sighed and looked up to find Elizabeth Johnston's dark intelligent eyes watching him.

On an impulse, he said, 'Tell me, Miss Johnston, have you ever had a feeling—an impression—of something *wrong* about this place?'

She looked surprised.

'In what way—wrong?'

'I couldn't really say. I'm thinking of something Miss Sally Finch said to me.'

'Oh—Sally Finch!'

There was an intonation in her voice which he found hard to place. He felt interested and went on:

'Miss Finch seemed to me a good observer, both shrewd and practical. She was very insistent on there being some-thing—odd, about this place—though she found it difficult to define just what it was.'

Elizabeth said sharply:

'That is her American way of thought. They are all the same, these Americans, nervous, apprehensive, suspecting every kind of foolish thing! Look at the fools they make of themselves with their witch hunts, their hysterical spy mania, their obsession over Communism. Sally Finch is typical.'

The inspector's interest grew. So Elizabeth disliked Sally Finch. Why? Because Sally was an American? Or did Elizabeth dislike Americans merely because Sally Finch was an American, and had she some reason of her own for disliking the attractive redhead? Perhaps it was just simple female jealousy.

He resolved to try a line of approach that he had sometimes found useful. He said smoothly:

'As you may appreciate, Miss Johnston, in an establishment like this, the level of intelligence varies a great deal. Some people—most people, we just ask for facts. But when we come across someone with a high level of intelligence—'

He paused. The inference was flattering. Would she respond?

After a brief pause, she did.

'I think I understand what you mean, Inspector. The intellectual level here is not, as you say, very high. Nigel Chapman has a certain quickness of intellect, but his mind is shallow. Leonard Bateson is a plodder—no more. Valerie Hobhouse has a good quality of mind, but her outlook is commercial, and she's too lazy to use her brains on anything worth while. What you want is the detachment of a trained mind.'

'Such as yours, Miss Johnston.'

She accepted the tribute without a protest. He realised, with some interest, that behind her modest pleasant manner, here was a young woman who was positively arrogant in her appraisement of her own qualities.

'I'm inclined to agree with your estimate of your fellow students, Miss Johnston. Chapman is clever but childish. Valerie Hobhouse has brains but a *blasé* attitude to life. You, as you say, have a trained mind. That's why I'd value your views—the views of a powerful detached intellect.'

For a moment he was afraid he had overdone it, but he need have had no fears.

'There is nothing wrong about this place, Inspector. Pay

no attention to Sally Finch. This is a decent well run hostel. I am certain that you will find no trace here of any subversive activities.'

Inspector Sharpe felt a little surprised.

'It wasn't really subversive activities I was thinking about.'

'Oh—I see—' She was a little taken aback. 'I was linking up what Celia said about a passport. But looking at it impartially and weighing up all the evidence, it seems quite certain to me that the reason for Celia's death was what I should express as a private one—some sex complication, perhaps. I'm sure it had nothing to do with what I might call the hostel as a hostel, or anything "going on" here. Nothing, I am sure, is going on. I should be aware of the fact if it were so, my perceptions are very keen.'

'I see. Well, thank you, Miss Johnston. You've been very kind and helpful.'

Elizabeth Johnston went out. Inspector Sharpe sat staring at the closed door and Sergeant Cobb had to speak to him twice before he roused himself.

'Eh?'

'I said that's the lot, sir.'

'Yes, and what have we got? Precious little. But I'll tell you one thing, Cobb. I'm coming back here to-morrow with a search warrant. We'll go away talking pretty now and they'll think it's all over. *But there's something going on in this place.* To-morrow I'll turn it upside down—not so easy when you don't know what you're looking for, but there's a chance that I'll find something to give me a clue. That's a very interesting girl who just went out. She's got the ego of a Napoleon, and I strongly suspect that she knows something.'

CHAPTER TWELVE

Hercule Poirot, at work upon his correspondence, paused in the middle of a sentence that he was dictating. Miss Lemon looked up questioningly.

'Yes, M. Poirot?'

'My mind wanders!' Poirot waved a hand. 'After all, this letter is not important. Be so kind, Miss Lemon, as to get me your sister upon the telephone.'

'Yes, M. Poirot.'

A few moments later Poirot crossed the room and took the receiver from his secretary's hand.

' 'Allo!' he said.

'Yes, M. Poirot?'

Mrs Hubbard sounded rather breathless.

'I trust, Mrs Hubbard, that I am not disturbing you?'

'I'm past being disturbed,' said Mrs Hubbard.

'There have been agitations, yes?' Poirot asked delicately.

'That's a very nice way of putting it, M. Poirot. That's exactly what they have been. Inspector Sharpe finished questioning all the students yesterday, and then he came back with a search warrant to-day and I've got Mrs Nicoletis on my hands with raving hysterics.'

Poirot clucked his tongue sympathetically.

Then he said, 'It is just a little question I have to ask. You sent me a list of those things that had disappeared—and other queer happenings—what I have to ask is this, did you write that list in chronological order?'

'You mean?'

'I mean, were the things written down exactly in the order of their disappearance?'

'No, they weren't. I'm sorry—I just put them down as I thought of them. I'm so sorry if I've misled you.'

'I should have asked you before,' said Poirot. 'But it did not strike me then as important. I have your list here. One evening shoe, bracelet, diamond ring, powder compact, lipstick, stethoscope, and so on. But you say that that was not the order of disappearance?'

'No.'

'Can you remember now, or would it be too difficult for you, what was the proper order?'

'Well, I'm not sure if I could now, M. Poirot. You see it's all some time ago. I should have to think it out. Actually, after I had talked with my sister and knew I was coming to see you, I made a list, and I should say that I put it down in the order of the things as I remembered them. I mean, the evening shoe because it was so peculiar; and then the bracelet and the powder compact and the cigarette lighter and the diamond ring because they were all rather important things and looked as though we had a genuine thief at work; and then I remembered the other more unimportant things later and added them. I mean the boracic and the electric light bulbs and the rucksack. They weren't really important and I only really thought of them as a kind of afterthought.'

'I see,' said Poirot. 'Yes, I see . . . Now what I would ask of you, madame, is to sit down now, when you have the leisure, that is . . .'

'I dare say when I've got Mrs Nicoletis to bed with a sedative and calmed down Geronimo and Maria, I shall have a little time. What is it you want me to do?'

'Sit down and try to put down, as nearly as you can, the chronological order in which the various incidents occurred.'

'Certainly, Monsieur Poirot. The rucksack, I believe was the first, and the electric light bulbs—which I really didn't think had any connection with the other things—and then the bracelet and the compact, no—the evening shoe. But there, you don't want to hear me speculate about it. I'll put them down as best I can.'

'Thank you, madame. I shall be much obliged to you.'

Poirot hung up the phone.

'I am vexed with myself,' he said to Miss Lemon. 'I have departed from the principles of order and method. I should have made quite sure from the start, the exact order in which these thefts occurred.'

'Dear, dear,' said Miss Lemon mechanically. 'Are you going to finish these letters now, M. Poirot?'

But once again Poirot waved her impatiently away.

II

On arrival back at Hickory Road with a search warrant on Saturday morning, Inspector Sharpe had demanded an interview with Mrs Nicoletis, who always came on Saturdays to do accounts with Mrs Hubbard. He had explained what he was about to do.

Mrs Nicoletis protested with vigour.

'But it is an insult, that! My students they will leave—they will all leave. I shall be ruined . . .'

'No, no, madam. I'm sure they will be sensible. After all, this is a case of murder.'

'It is not murder—it is suicide.'

'And I'm sure once I've explained, no one will object . . .'

Mrs Hubbard put in a soothing word.

'I'm sure,' she said, 'everyone will be sensible—except,' she added thoughtfully, 'perhaps Mr Achmed Ali and Mr Chandra Lal.'

'Pah!' said Mrs Nicoletis. 'Who cares about them?'

'Thank you, madam,' said the inspector. 'Then I'll make a start here, in your sitting-room.'

An immediate and violent protest came from Mrs Nicoletis at the suggestion.

'You search where you please,' she said, 'but here, no! I refuse.'

'I'm sorry, Mrs Nicoletis, but I have to go through the house from top to bottom.'

'That is right, yes, but not in my room. I am above the law.'

'No one's above the law. I'm afraid I shall have to ask you to stand aside.'

'It is an outrage,' Mrs Nicoletis screamed with fury. 'You are officious busybodies. I will write to everyone. I will write to my member of Parliament. I will write to the papers.'

'Write to anyone you please, madam,' said Inspector Sharpe, 'I'm going to search this room.'

He started straight away upon the bureau. A large carton of confectionery, a mass of papers, and a large variety of assorted junk rewarded his search. He moved from there to a cupboard in the corner of the room.

'This is locked. Can I have the key, please?'

'Never!' screamed Mrs Nicoletis. 'Never, never, never shall you have the key! Beast and pig of a policeman, I spit at you. I spit! I spit! I spit!'

'You might just as well give me the key,' said Inspector Sharpe. 'If not, I shall simply prise the door open.'

'I will not give you the key! You will have to tear my clothes off me before you get the key! And that—*that* will be a scandal.'

'Get a chisel, Cobb,' said Inspector Sharpe resignedly.

Mrs Nicoletis uttered a scream of fury. Inspector Sharpe paid no attention. The chisel was brought. Two sharp cracks and the door of the cupboard came open. As it swung forward a large consignment of empty brandy bottles poured out of the cupboard.

'Beast! Pig! Devil!' screamed Mrs Nicoletis.

'Thank you, madam,' said the inspector politely. 'We've finished in here.'

Mrs Hubbard tactfully replaced the bottles while Mrs Nicoletis had hysterics.

One mystery, the mystery of Mrs Nicoletis's tempers, was now cleared up.

III

Poirot's telephone call came through just as Mrs Hubbard was pouring out an appropriate dose of sedative from the private medicine cupboard in her sitting-room. After replacing the receiver she went back to Mrs Nicoletis whom she had left screaming and kicking her heels on the sofa in her own sitting-room.

'Now you drink this,' said Mrs Hubbard. 'And you'll feel better.'

'Gestapo!' said Mrs Nicoletis, who was now quiet but sullen.

'I shouldn't think any more about it if I were you,' said Mrs Hubbard soothingly.

'Gestapo!' said Mrs Nicoletis again. 'Gestapo! That is what they are!'

'They have to do their duty, you know,' said Mrs Hubbard.

'Is it their duty to pry into my private cupboards? I say to them, "That is not for you." I lock it. I put the key down my bosom. If you had not been there as a witness they would have torn my clothes off me without shame.'

'Oh no, I don't think they would have done *that*,' said Mrs Hubbard.

'That is what *you* say! Instead they get a chisel and they force my door. That is structural damage to the house for which *I* shall be responsible.'

'Well, you see, if you wouldn't give them the key . . .'

'Why should I give them the key? It is *my* key. My private key. And this is my private room. My private room and I say to the police, "Keep out" and they do *not* keep out.'

'Well, after all, Mrs Nicoletis, there has been a murder, remember. And after a murder one has to put up with certain things which might not be very pleasant at ordinary times.'

'I spit upon the murder!' said Mrs Nicoletis. 'That little Celia she commits suicide. She has a silly love affair and she takes poison. It is the sort of thing that is always happening. They are so stupid about love, these girls—as though love mattered! One year, two years and it is all finished, the grand passion! The man is the same as any other man! But these silly girls they do not know that. They take the sleeping draught and the disinfectant and they turn on gas taps and then it is too late.'

'Well,' said Mrs Hubbard, turning full circle, as it were,

to where the conversation had started, 'I shouldn't worry any more about it all now.'

'That is all very well for *you*. Me, I have to worry. It is not safe for me any longer.'

'Safe?' Mrs Hubbard looked at her, startled.

'It was my private cupboard,' Mrs Nicoletis insisted. 'Nobody knows what was in my private cupboard. I did not want them to know. And now they *do* know. I am very uneasy. They may think—what will they think?'

'Who do you mean by *they*?'

Mrs Nicoletis shrugged her large, handsome shoulders and looked sulky.

'You do not understand,' she said, 'but it makes me uneasy. Very uneasy.'

'You'd better tell me,' said Mrs Hubbard. 'Then perhaps I can help you.'

'Thank goodness I do not sleep here,' said Mrs Nicoletis. 'These locks on the doors here they are all alike; one key fits any other. No, thanks to heaven, I do not sleep here.'

Mrs Hubbard said:

'Mrs Nicoletis, if you are afraid of something, hadn't you better tell me just what it is?'

Mrs Nicoletis gave her a flickering look from her dark eyes and then looked away again.

'You have said it yourself,' she said evasively. 'You have said there has been murder in this house, so naturally one is uneasy. Who may be next? One does not even know who the murderer is. That is because the police are so stupid, or perhaps they have been bribed.'

'That's all nonsense and you know it,' said Mrs Hubbard. 'But tell me, have you got any cause for real anxiety . . .?'

Mrs Nicoletis flew into one of her tempers.

'Ah, *you* do not think I have any cause for anxiety? You know best as usual! You know everything! You are so wonderful; you cater, you manage, you spend money like water on food so that the students are fond of you, and now you want to manage *my* affairs! But that, no! I keep my affairs to myself and nobody shall pry into them, do you hear? No, Mrs What-do-you-call-it Paul Pry.'

'Please yourself,' said Mrs Hubbard exasperated.

'You are a spy—I always knew it.'

'A spy on what?'

'Nothing,' said Mrs Nicoletis. 'There is nothing here to spy upon. If you think there is it is because you made it up. If lies are told about me I shall know who told them.'

'If you wish me to leave,' said Mrs Hubbard, 'you've only got to say so.'

'No, you are not to leave. I forbid it. Not at this moment. Not when I have all the cares of the police, of murder, of everything else on my hands. I shall not allow you to abandon me.'

'Oh, all right,' said Mrs Hubbard helplessly. 'But really, it's very difficult to know what you do want. Sometimes I don't think you know yourself. You'd better lie down on my bed and have a sleep——'

CHAPTER THIRTEEN

Hercule Poirot alighted from a taxi at 26 Hickory Road.

The door was opened to him by Geronimo who welcomed him as an old friend. There was a constable standing in the hall and Geronimo drew Poirot into the dining-room and closed the door.

'It is terrible,' he whispered, as he assisted Poirot off with his overcoat. 'We have police here all time! Ask questions, go here, go there, look in cupboards, look in drawers, come into Maria's kitchen even. Maria very angry. She says she like to hit policeman with rolling-pin but I say better not. I say policeman not like being hit by rolling-pins and they make us more embarrassments if Maria do that.'

'You have the good sense,' said Poirot approvingly. 'Is Mrs Hubbard at liberty?'

'I take you upstairs to her.'

'A little moment.' Poirot stopped him. 'Do you remember the day when certain electric light bulbs disappeared?'

'Oh yes, I remember. But that long time ago now. One —two—three months ago.'

'Exactly what electric light bulbs were taken?'

'The one in the hall and I think in the common-room. Someone make joke. Take all the bulbs out.'

'You don't remember the exact date?'

Geronimo struck an attitude as he thought.

'I do not remember,' he said. 'But I think it was on day when policeman come, some time in February—'

'A policeman? What did a policeman come here for?'

'He come here to see Mrs Nicoletis about a student. Very bad student, come from Africa. Not do work. Go to labour exchange, get National Assistance, then have woman and she go out with men for him. Very bad that. Police not like that. All this in Manchester, I think, or Sheffield. So he ran away from there and he come here, but police come after him and they talk to Mrs Hubbard about him. Yes. And she say he not stop here because she no like him and she send him away.'

'I see. They were trying to trace him.'

'Scusi?'

'They were trying to find him?'

'Yes, yes, that is right. They find him and then they put him in prison because he live on woman, and live on woman must not do. This is nice house here. Nothing like that *here*.'

'And that was the day the bulbs were missing?'

'Yes. Because I turn switch and nothing happen. And I go into common-room and no bulb there, and I look in drawer here for spares and I see bulbs have been taken away. So I go down to kitchen and ask Maria if she know where spare bulbs—but she angry because she not like police come and she say spare bulbs not her business, so I bring just candles.'

Poirot digested this story as he followed Geronimo up the stairs to Mrs Hubbard's room.

Poirot was welcomed warmly by Mrs Hubbard, who was looking tired and harassed. She held out, at once, a piece of paper to him.

'I've done my best, M. Poirot, to write down these things in the proper order but I wouldn't like to say that it's a hundred per cent accurate now. You see, it's very difficult when you look back over a period of months to remember just when this, that or the other happened.'

'I am deeply grateful to you, madame. And how is Mrs Nicoletis?'

'I've given her a sedative and I hope she's asleep now. She made a terrible fuss over the search warrant. She refused to open the cupboard in her room and the inspector broke it open and quantities of empty brandy bottles tumbled out.'

'Ah!' said Poirot, making a tactful sound.

'Which really explains quite a lot of things,' said Mrs Hubbard. 'I really can't imagine why I didn't think of that before, having seen as much of drink as I have out in

Singapore. But all that, I'm sure, isn't what interests you.'

'Everything interests me,' said Poirot.

He sat down and studied the piece of paper that Mrs Hubbard had handed to him.

'Ah!' he said, after a moment or two. 'I see that now the rucksack heads the list.'

'Yes. It wasn't a very important thing, but I do remember now, definitely, that it happened before the jewellery and those sort of things began to disappear. It was all rather mixed up with some trouble we had about one of the coloured students. He'd left a day or two before this happened and I remember thinking that it might have been a revengeful act on his part before he went. There'd been, well—a little trouble.'

'Ah! Geronimo has recounted to me something like that. You had, I believe, the police here? Is that right?'

'Yes. It seems they had an inquiry from Sheffield or Birmingham or somewhere. It had all been rather a scandal. Immoral earnings and all that sort of thing. He was had up about it in court later. Actually, he'd only stayed here about three or four days. Then I didn't like his behaviour, the way he was carrying on, so I told him that his room was engaged and that he'd have to go. I wasn't really at all surprised when the police called. Of course, I couldn't tell them where he'd gone to, but they got on his track all right.'

'And it was after that that you found the rucksack?'

'Yes, I think so—it's hard to remember. You see, Len Bateson was going off on a hitch-hike and he couldn't find his rucksack anywhere and he created a terrible fuss about it, and everyone did a lot of searching, and at last Geronimo found it shoved behind the boiler all cut to ribbons. Such an odd thing to happen. So curious; and pointless, M. Poirot.'

'Yes,' Poirot agreed. 'Curious and pointless.'

He remained thoughtful for a moment.

'And it was on that same day, the day that the police came to inquire about this African student, that some electric bulbs disappeared—or so Geronimo tells me. Was it that day?'

'Well, I really can't remember. Yes, yes, I think you're

right, because I remember coming downstairs with the police inspector and going into the common-room with him and there were candles there. We wanted to ask Akibombo whether this other young man had spoken to him at all or told him where he was going to stay.'

'Who else was in the common-room?'

'Oh, I think most of the students had come back by that time. It was in the evening, you know, just about six o'clock. I asked Geronimo about the bulbs and he said they'd been taken out. I asked him why he hadn't replaced them and he said we were right out of electric bulbs. I was rather annoyed as it seemed such a silly pointless joke. I thought of it as a joke, not as stealing, but I was surprised that we had no more electric bulbs because we usually keep quite a good supply in stock. Still, I didn't take it seriously, M. Poirot, not at that time.'

'The bulbs and the rucksack,' said Poirot thoughtfully.

'But it still seems to me possible,' said Mrs Hubbard, 'that those two things have no connection with poor little Celia's peccadilloes. You remember she denied very earnestly that she'd ever touched the rucksack at all.'

'Yes, yes, that is true. How soon after this did the thefts begin?'

'Oh dear, M. Poirot, you've no idea how difficult all this is to remember. Let me see—that was March, no, February —the end of February. Yes, yes, I think Genevieve said she'd missed her bracelet about a week after that. Yes, between the 20th and 25th of February.'

'And after that the thefts went on fairly continuously?'

'Yes.'

'And this rucksack was Len Bateson's?'

'Yes.'

'And he was very annoyed about it?'

'Well, you mustn't go by that, M. Poirot,' said Mrs Hubbard, smiling a little. 'Len Bateson is that kind of boy, you know. Warm hearted, generous, kind to a fault, but one of those fiery, outspoken tempers.'

'What was it, this rucksack—something special?'

'Oh no, it was just the ordinary kind.'

'Could you show me one like it?'

'Well, yes, of course. Colin's got one, I think, just like it. So has Nigel—in fact Len's got one again now because he had to go and buy another. The students usually buy them at the shop at the end of the road. It's a very good place for all kinds of camping equipment and hikers' outfits. Shorts, sleeping-bags, all that sort of thing. And very cheap —much cheaper than any of the big stores.'

'If I could just see one of these rucksacks, madame?'

Mrs Hubbard obligingly led him to Colin McNabb's room.

Colin himself was not there, but Mrs Hubbard opened the wardrobe, stooped, and picked up a rucksack which she held out to Poirot.

'There you are, M. Poirot. That's exactly like the one that was missing and that we found all cut up.'

'It would take some cutting,' murmured Poirot, as he fingered the rucksack appreciatively. 'One could not snip at this with a little pair of embroidery scissors.'

'Oh no, it wasn't what you'd expect a—well, a girl to do, for instance. There must have been a certain amount of strength involved, I should say. Strength and—well— malice, you know.'

'I know, yes, I know. It is not pleasant. Not pleasant to think about.'

'Then, when later that scarf of Valerie's was found, also slashed to pieces, well, it did look—what shall I say—un-balanced.'

'Ah,' said Poirot. 'But I think there you are wrong, madame. I do not think there is anything unbalanced about this business. I think it has aim and purpose, and shall we say, method?'

'Well, I dare say you know more about these things, M. Poirot, than I do,' said Mrs Hubbard. 'All I can say is, I don't like it. As far as I can judge we've got a very nice lot of students here and it would distress me very much to think that one of them is—well, not what I'd like to think he or she is.'

Poirot had wandered over to the window. He opened it and stepped out on to the old-fashioned balcony.

The room looked out over the back of the house. Below was a small, sooty garden.

'It is more quiet here than at the front, I expect?' he said.

'In a way. But Hickory Road isn't really a noisy road. And facing this way you get all the cats at night. Yowling, you know, and knocking the lids off the dustbins.'

Poirot looked down at four large battered ash-cans and other assorted backyard junk.

'Where is the boiler-house?'

'That's the door to it, down there next to the coal-house.'

'I see.'

He gazed down speculatively.

'Who else has rooms facing this way?'

'Nigel Chapman and Len Bateson have the next room to this.'

'And beyond them?'

'Then it's the next house—and the girls' rooms. First the room Celia had and beyond it Elizabeth Johnston's and then Patricia Lane's. Valerie and Jean Tomlinson look out to the front.'

Poirot nodded and came back into the room.

'He is neat, this young man,' he murmured, looking round him appreciatively.

'Yes. Colin's room is always very tidy. Some of the boys live in a terrible mess,' said Mrs Hubbard. 'You should see Len Bateson's room.' She added indulgently, 'But he is a nice boy, M. Poirot.'

'You say that these rucksacks are bought at the shop at the end of the road?'

'Yes.'

'What is the name of that shop?'

'Now really, M. Poirot, when you ask me like that I can't remember. Mabberley, I think. Or else Kelso. No, I know they don't sound the same kind of name but they're the same sort of name in my mind. Really, of course, because I knew some people once called Kelso and some other ones called Mabberley, and they were very alike.'

'Ah,' said Poirot. 'That is one of the reasons for things that always fascinate me. The unseen link.'

He looked once more out of the window and down into the garden, then took his leave of Mrs Hubbard and left the house.

He walked down Hickory Road until he came to the corner and turned into the main road. He had no difficulty in recognising the shop of Mrs Hubbard's description. It displayed in great profusion picnic baskets, rucksacks, Thermos flasks, sports equipment of all kinds, shorts, bush shirts, topees, tents, swimming suits, bicycle lamps and torches; in fact all possible needs of young and athletic youth. The name above the shop, he noted, was neither Mabberley nor Kelso but Hicks. After a careful study of the goods displayed in the window, Poirot entered and represented himself as desirous of purchasing a rucksack for a hypothetical nephew.

'He makes "le camping," you understand,' said Poirot at his most foreign. 'He goes with other students upon the feet and all he needs he takes with him on his back, and the cars and the lorries that pass, they give him a lift.'

The proprietor, who was a small, obliging man with sandy hair, replied promptly.

'Ah, hitch-hiking,' he said. 'They all do it nowadays. Must lose the buses and the railways a lot of money, though. Hitch-hike themselves all over Europe some of these young people do. Now it's a rucksack you're wanting, sir. Just an ordinary rucksack?'

'I understand so. Yes. You have a variety then?'

'Well, we have one or two extra light ones for ladies, but this is the general article we sell. Good, stout, stand a lot of wear, and really very cheap though I say it myself.'

He produced a stout canvas affair which was, as far as Poirot could judge, an exact replica of the one he had been shown in Colin's room. Poirot examined it, asked a few more exotic and unnecessary questions, and ended by paying for it then and there.

'Ah yes, we sell a lot of these,' said the man as he made

it up into a parcel.

'A good many students lodge round here, do they not?'

'Yes. This is a neighbourhood with a lot of students.'

'There is one hostel, I believe in Hickory Road?'

'Oh yes, I've sold several to the young gentlemen there. And the young ladies. They usually come here for any equipment they want before they go off. My prices are cheaper than the big stores, and so I tell them. There you are, sir, and I'm sure your nephew will be delighted with the service he gets out of this.'

Poirot thanked him and went out with his parcel.

He had only gone a step or two when a hand fell on his shoulder.

It was Inspector Sharpe.

'Just the man I want to see,' said Sharpe.

'You have accomplished your search of the house?'

'I've searched the house, but I don't know that I've accomplished very much. There's a place along here where you can get a very decent sandwich and a cup of coffee. Come along with me if you're not busy. I'd like to talk to you.'

The sandwich bar was almost empty. The two men carried their plates and cups to a small table in a corner.

Here Sharpe recounted the results of his questioning of the students.

'The only person we've got any evidence against is young Chapman,' he said. 'And there we've got too much. Three lots of poison through his hands! But there's no reason to believe he'd any animus against Celia Austin, and I doubt if he'd have been as frank about his activities if he was really guilty.'

'It opens out other possibilities, though.'

'Yes—all that stuff knocking about in a drawer. Silly young ass!'

He went on to Elizabeth Johnston and her account of what Celia had said to her.

'If what she said is true, it's significant.'

'Very significant,' Poirot agreed.

The inspector quoted:

' "I shall know more about it to-morrow." '

'And so—to-morrow never came for that poor girl. Your search of the house—did it accomplish anything?'

'There were one or two things that were—what shall I say?—unexpected, perhaps.'

'Such as?'

'Elizabeth Johnston is a member of the Communist Party. We found her Party card.'

'Yes,' said Poirot, thoughtfully. 'That is interesting.'

'You wouldn't have expected it,' said Inspector Sharpe. 'I didn't until I questioned her yesterday. She's got a lot of personality, that girl.'

'I should think she was a valuable recruit to the Party,' said Hercule Poirot. 'She is a young woman of quite unusual intelligence, I should say.'

'It was interesting to me,' said Inspector Sharpe, 'because she has never paraded those sympathies, apparently. She's kept very quiet about it at Hickory Road. I don't see that it has any significance in connection with the case of Celia Austin, I mean—but it's a thing to bear in mind.'

'What else did you find?'

Inspector Sharpe shrugged his shoulders.

'Miss Patricia Lane, in her drawer, had a handkerchief rather extensively stained with green ink.'

Poirot's eyebrows rose.

'Green ink? Patricia Lane! So it may have been she who took the ink and spilled it over Elizabeth Johnston's papers and then wiped her hands afterwards. But surely . . .'

'Surely she wouldn't want her dear Nigel to be suspected,' Sharpe finished for him.

'One would not have thought so. Of course, someone else might have put the handkerchief in her drawer.'

'Likely enough.'

'Anything else?'

'Well,' Sharpe reflected for a moment. 'It seems Leonard Bateson's father is in Longwith Vale Mental Hospital, a certified patient. I don't suppose it's of any particular interest, but . . .'

'But Len Bateson's father is insane. Probably without

significance, as you say, but it is a fact to be stored away in the memory. It would even be interesting to know what particular form his mania takes.'

'Bateson's a nice young fellow,' said Sharpe, 'but of course his temper is a bit, well, uncontrolled.'

Poirot nodded. Suddenly, vividly, he remembered Celia Austin saying, 'Of course, I wouldn't cut up a rucksack. Anyway that was only temper.' How did she know it was temper? Had she seen Len Bateson hacking at that rucksack? He came back to the present to hear Sharpe say, with a grin:

'. . . and Mr Achmed Ali has some extremely pornographic literature and postcards which explains why *he* went up in the air over the search.'

'There were many protests, no doubt?'

'I should say there were. A French girl practically had hysterics and an Indian, Mr Chandra Lal, threatened to make an international incident of it. There were a few subversive pamphlets amongst *his* belongings—the usual half-baked stuff—and one of the West Africans had some rather fearsome souvenirs and fetishes. Yes, a search warrant certainly shows you the peculiar side of human nature. You heard about Mrs Nicoletis and her private cupboard?'

'Yes, I heard about that.'

Inspector Sharpe grinned.

'Never seen so many empty brandy bottles in my life! And was she mad at us!'

He laughed, and then, abruptly, became serious.

'But we didn't find what we went after,' he said. 'No passports except strictly legitimate ones.'

'You can hardly expect such a thing as a false passport to be left about for you to find, *mon ami*. You never had occasion, did you, to make an official visit to 26 Hickory Road in connection with a passport? Say, in the last six months?'

'No. I'll tell you the only occasions on which we did call round—within the times you mention.'

He detailed them carefully.

Poirot listened with a frown.

'All that, it does not make sense,' he said.

He shook his head.

'Things will only make sense if we begin at the beginning.'

'What do you call the beginning, Poirot?'

'The rucksack, my friend,' said Poirot softly. 'The rucksack. All this began with a rucksack.'

CHAPTER FOURTEEN

Mrs Nicoletis came up the stairs from the basement, where she had just succeeded in thoroughly infuriating both Geronimo and the temperamental Maria.

'Liars and thieves,' said Mrs Nicoletis, in a loud triumphant voice. 'All Italians are liars and thieves!'

Mrs Hubbard, who was just descending the stairs, gave a short vexed sigh.

'It's a pity,' she said, 'to upset them just while they're cooking the supper.'

Mrs Hubbard suppressed the retort that rose to her lips.

'I shall come in as usual on Monday,' said Mrs Nicoletis.

'Yes, Mrs Nicoletis.'

'And please get someone to repair my cupboard door first thing Monday morning. The bill for repairing it will go to the police, do you understand? To the police.'

Mrs Hubbard looked dubious.

'And I want fresh electric light bulbs put in the dark passages—stronger ones. The passages are too dark.'

'You said especially that you wanted low power bulbs in the passages—for economy.'

'That was last week,' snapped Mrs Nicoletis. 'Now—it is different. Now I look over my shoulder—and I wonder "Who is following me?"'

Was her employer dramatising herself, Mrs Hubbard wondered, or was she really afraid of something or someone? Mrs Nicoletis had such a habit of exaggerating everything that it was always hard to know how much reliance to place on her statements.

Mrs Hubbard said doubtfully:

'Are you sure you ought to go home by yourself? Would you like me to come with you?'

'I shall be safer there than here, I can tell you!'

'But what is it you are afraid of? If I knew, perhaps I could—'

'It is not your business. I tell you nothing. I find it insupportable the way you continually ask me questions.'

'I'm sorry, I'm sure—'

'Now you are offended.' Mrs Nicoletis gave her a beaming smile. 'I am bad tempered and rude—yes. But I have much to worry me. And remember I trust you and rely on you. What I should do without you, dear Mrs Hubbard, I really do not know. See, I kiss my hand to you. Have a pleasant week-end. Good night.'

Mrs Hubbard watched her as she went out through the front door and pulled it to behind her. Relieving her feelings with a rather inadequate 'Well, really!' Mrs Hubbard turned towards the kitchen stairs.

Mrs Nicoletis went down the front steps, out through the gate and turned to the left. Hickory Road was a fairly broad road. The houses in it were set back a little in their gardens. At the end of the road, a few minutes' walk from number 26, was one of London's main thoroughfares, down which buses were roaring. There were traffic lights at the end of the road and a public-house, The Queen's Necklace, at the corner. Mrs Nicoletis walked in the middle of the pavement and from time to time sent a nervous glance over her shoulder, but there was no one in sight. Hickory Road appeared to be unusually deserted this evening. She quickened her steps a little as she drew near The Queen's Necklace. Taking another hasty glance round she slipped rather guiltily through into the saloon bar.

Sipping the double brandy that she had asked for, her spirits revived. She no longer looked the frightened and uneasy woman that she had a short time previously. Her animosity against the police, however, was not lessened. She murmured under her breath, 'Gestapo! I shall make them pay. Yes, they shall pay!' and finished off her drink. She ordered another and brooded over recent happenings. Unfortunate, extremely unfortunate, that the police should have been so tactless as to discover her secret hoard, and too much to hope that word would not get around amongst the students and the rest of them. Mrs Hubbard would be discreet, perhaps, or again perhaps not, because really, could one trust anyone? These things always did get round. Geronimo knew. He had probably already told his wife, and she would tell the cleaning women and so it would go on until—she started violently as a voice behind her said:

'Why, Mrs Nick, I didn't know this was a haunt of yours?'

She wheeled round sharply and then gave a sigh of relief.

'Oh, it's you,' she said. 'I thought . . .'

'Who did you think it was? The big bad wolf? What are you drinking? Have another on me.'

'It is all the worry,' Mrs Nicoletis explained with dignity. 'These policemen searching my house, upsetting everyone. My poor heart. I have to be very careful with my heart. I do not care for drink, but really I felt quite faint outside. I thought a little brandy . . .'

'Nothing like brandy. Here you are.'

Mrs Nicoletis left The Queen's Necklace a short while later feeling revived and positively happy. She would not take a bus, she decided. It was such a fine night and the air would be good for her. Yes, definitely the air would be good for her. She felt not exactly unsteady on her feet but just a little bit uncertain. One brandy less, perhaps, would have been wise, but the air would soon clear her head. After all, why shouldn't a lady have a quiet drink in her own room from time to time? What was there wrong with it? It was not as though she had ever allowed herself to be seen intoxicated. Intoxicated? Of course, she was never intoxicated. And anyway, if they didn't like it; if they ticked her off, she'd soon tell them where they got off! *She* knew a thing or two, didn't she? If she liked to shoot off her mouth! Mrs Nicoletis tossed her head in a bellicose manner and swerved abruptly to avoid a pillar-box which had advanced upon her in a menacing manner. No doubt, her head *was* swimming a little. Perhaps if she just leant against the wall here for a little? If she closed her eyes for a moment or two. . . .

Police-Constable Bott, swinging magnificently down on his beat, was accosted by a timid-looking clerk.

'There's a woman here, Officer. I really—she seems to have been taken ill or something. She's lying in a heap.'

Police-Constable Bott bent his energetic steps that way, and stooped over the recumbent form. A strong aroma of brandy confirmed his suspicions.

'Passed out,' he said. 'Drunk. Ah well, don't worry, sir, we'll see to it.'

II

Hercule Poirot, having finished his Sunday breakfast, wiped his moustaches carefully free from all traces of his breakfast cup of chocolate and passed into his sitting-room.

Neatly arranged on the table were four rucksacks, each with its bill attached—the result of instructions given to George. Poirot took the rucksack he had purchased the day before from its wrapping, and added it to the others. The result was interesting. The rucksack he had bought from Mr Hicks did not seem inferior in any way that he could see, to the articles purchased by George from various other establishments. But it was very decidedly cheaper.

'Interesting,' said Hercule Poirot.

He stared at the rucksacks.

Then he examined them in detail. Inside and outside, turning them upside down, feeling the seams, the pockets, the handles. Then he rose, went into the bathroom and came back with a small sharp corn-knife. Turning the rucksack he had bought at Mr Hicks's store inside out, he attacked the bottom of it with the knife. Between the inner lining and the bottom there was a heavy piece of corrugated stiffening, rather resembling in appearance corrugated paper. Poirot looked at the dismembered rucksack with a great deal of interest.

Then he proceeded to attack the other rucksacks.

He sat back finally and surveyed the amount of destruction he had just accomplished.

Then he drew the telephone towards him and after a short delay managed to get through to Inspector Sharpe.

'*Ecoutez, mon cher,*' he said. 'I want to know just two things.'

Something in the nature of a guffaw came from Inspector Sharpe.

'*I know two things about the horse,*
  And one of them is rather coarse,' he observed.

'I beg your pardon,' said Hercule Poirot, surprised.

'Nothing. Nothing. Just a rhyme I used to know. What are the two things you want to know?'

'You mentioned yesterday certain police inquiries at Hickory Road made during the last three months. Can you tell me the dates of them and also the time of day they were made?'

'Yes—well—that should be easy. It'll be in the files. Just wait and I'll look it up.'

It was not long before the inspector returned to the phone. 'First inquiry as to Indian student disseminating subversive propaganda, 18th December last—3.30 p.m.'

'That is too long ago.'

'Inquiry *re* Montagu Jones, Eurasian, wanted in connection with murder of Mrs Alice Combe of Cambridge—February 24th—5.30 p.m. Inquiry *re* William Robinson—native West Africa, wanted by Sheffield police—March 6th, 11 a.m.'

'Ah! I thank you.'

'But if you think that either of those cases could have any connection with—'

Poirot interrupted him.

'No, they have no connection. I am interested only in the time of day they were made.'

'What *are* you up to, Poirot?'

'I dissect rucksacks, my friend. It is very interesting.'

Gently he replaced the receiver.

He took from his pocket-book the amended list that Mrs Hubbard had handed him the day before. It ran as follows:

Rucksack (Len Bateson's)
Electric light bulbs
Bracelet (Genevieve's)
Diamond ring (Patricia's)

Powder compact (Genevieve's)
Evening shoe (Sally's)
Lipstick (Elizabeth Johnston's)
Ear-rings (Valerie's)
Stethoscope (Len Bateson's)
Bath salts (?)
Scarf cut in pieces (Valerie's)
Trousers (Colin's)
Cookery book (?)
Boracic (Chandra Lal's)
Costume brooch (Sally's)
Ink spilled on Elizabeth's notes.
(This is the best I can do. It's not absolutely accurate.
L. Hubbard.)

Poirot looked at it a long time.

He sighed and murmured to himself, 'Yes . . . decidedly
. . . we have to eliminate the things that do not matter. . . .'

He had an idea as to who could help him to do that. It
was Sunday. Most of the students would probably be at
home.

He dialled the number of 26 Hickory Road and asked to
speak to Miss Valerie Hobhouse. A thick rather guttural
voice seemed rather doubtful as to whether she was up yet,
but said it would go and see.

Presently he heard a low husky voice:

'Valerie Hobhouse speaking.'

'It is Hercule Poirot here. You remember me?'

'Of course, M. Poirot. What can I do for you?'

'I would like, if I may, to have a short conversation with
you?'

'Certainly.'

'I may come round, then, to Hickory Road?'

'Yes. I'll be expecting you. I'll tell Geronimo to bring you
up to my room. There's not much privacy here on a
Sunday.'

'Thank you, Miss Hobhouse. I am most grateful.'

Geronimo opened the door to Poirot with a flourish, then
bending forward he spoke with his usual conspiratorial air.

'I take you up to Miss Valerie very quietly. Hush sh sh.'

Placing his finger on his lips, he led the way upstairs and into a good sized room overlooking Hickory Road. It was furnished with taste and a reasonable amount of luxury as a bed-sitting-room. The divan bed was covered with a worn but beautiful Persian rug, and there was an attractive Queen Anne walnut bureau which Poirot judged hardly likely to be one of the original furnishings of 26 Hickory Road.

Valerie Hobhouse was standing ready to greet him. She looked tired, he thought, and there were dark circles round her eyes.

'*Mais vous êtes très bien ici,*' said Poirot, as he greeted her. 'It is *chic*. It has an air.'

Valerie smiled.

'I've been here a good time,' she said. 'Two and a half years. Nearly three. I've dug myself in more or less and I've got some of my own things.'

'You are not a student, are you, mademoiselle?'

'Oh no. Purely commercial. I've got a job.'

'In a—cosmetic firm, was it?'

'Yes. I'm one of the buyers for Sabrina Fair—it's a beauty salon. Actually I have a small share in the business. We run a certain amount of side-lines besides beauty treatment. Accessories, that type of thing. Small Parisian novelties. And that's my department.'

'You go over then fairly often to Paris and to the Continent?'

'Oh yes, about once a month, sometimes oftener.'

'You must forgive me,' said Poirot, 'if I seem to be displaying curiosity . . .'

'Why not?' She cut him short. 'In the circumstances in which we find ourselves we must all put up with curiosity. I've answered a good many questions yesterday from Inspector Sharpe. You look as though you would like an upright chair, Monsieur Poirot, rather than a low arm-chair.'

'You display the perspicacity, mademoiselle.' Poirot sat down carefully and squarely in a high-backed chair with arms to it.

Valerie sat down on the divan. She offered him a cigarette and took one herself and lighted it. He studied her with some attention. She had a nervous, rather haggard elegance that appealed to him more than mere conventional good looks would have done. An intelligent and attractive young woman, he thought. He wondered if her nervousness was the result of the recent inquiry or whether it was a natural component of her manner. He remembered that he had thought much the same about her on the evening when he had come to supper.

'Inspector Sharpe has been making inquiries of you?' he asked.

'Yes, indeed.'

'And you have told him all that you know?'

'Of course.'

'I wonder,' said Poirot, 'if that is true.'

She looked at him with an ironic expression.

'Since you did not hear my answers to Inspector Sharpe you can hardly be a judge,' she said.

'Ah no. It is merely one of my little ideas. I have them, you know—the little ideas. They are here.' He tapped his head.

It could be noticed that Poirot, as he sometimes did, was deliberately playing the mountebank. Valerie, however, did not smile. She looked at him in a straightforward manner. When she spoke it was with a certain abruptness.

'Shall we come to the point, M. Poirot?' she asked. 'I really don't know what you're driving at.'

'But certainly, Miss Hobhouse.'

He took from his pocket a little package.

'You can guess, perhaps, what I have here?'

'I'm not clairvoyant, M. Poirot. I can't see through paper and wrappings.'

'I have here,' said Poirot, 'the ring that was stolen from Miss Patricia Lane.'

'Patricia's engagement ring? I mean, her mother's engagement ring? But why should *you* have it?'

'I asked her to lend it to me for a day or two.'

Again Valerie's rather surprised eyebrows mounted her forehead.

'Indeed,' she observed.

'I was interested in the ring,' said Poirot. 'Interested in its disappearance, in its return and in something else about it. So I asked Miss Lane to lend it to me. She agreed readily. I took it straight away to a jeweller friend of mine.'

'Yes?'

'I asked him to report on the diamond in it. A fairly large stone, if you remember, flanked at either side by a little cluster of small stones. You remember—mademoiselle?'

'I think so. I don't really remember it very well.'

'But you handled it, didn't you? It was in your soup plate.'

'That was how it was returned! Oh yes, I remember that. I nearly swallowed it.' Valerie gave a short laugh.

'As I say, I took the ring to my jeweller friend and I asked him his opinion on the diamond. Do you know what his answer was?'

'How could I?'

'His answer was that the stone was not a diamond. It was merely a zircon. A white zircon.'

'Oh!' She stared at him. Then she went on, her tone a little uncertain, 'D'you mean that—Patricia thought it was a diamond but it was only a zircon or . . .'

Poirot was shaking his head.

'No, I do not mean that. It was the engagement ring, so I understand, of this Patricia Lane's mother. Miss Patricia Lane is a young lady of good family, and her people, I should say, certainly before recent taxation, were in comfortable circumstances. In those circles, mademoiselle, money is spent upon an engagement ring. An engagement ring must be a handsome ring—a *diamond* ring or a ring containing some other precious stone. I am quite certain that the papa of Miss Lane would not have given her mamma anything but a valuable engagement ring.'

'As to that,' said Valerie, 'I couldn't agree with you more. Patricia's father was a small country squire, I believe.'

'Therefore,' said Poirot, 'it would seem that the stone in the ring must have been replaced by another stone later.'

'I suppose,' said Valerie slowly, 'that Pat might have lost

the stone out of it, couldn't afford to replace it with a diamond, and had a zircon put in instead.'

'That is possible,' said Hercule Poirot, 'but I do not think it is what happened.'

'Well, M. Poirot, if we're guessing, what *do* you think happened.'

'I think,' said Poirot, 'that the ring was taken by Mademoiselle Celia and that the diamond was deliberately removed and the zircon substituted before the ring was returned.'

Valerie sat up very straight.

'You think Celia stole that diamond deliberately?'

Poirot shook his head.

'No,' he said. 'I think *you* stole it, mademoiselle.'

Valerie Hobhouse caught her breath sharply:

'Well, really!' she exclaimed. 'That seems to me pretty thick. You've no earthly evidence of any kind.'

'But, yes,' Poirot interrupted her. 'I have evidence. The ring was returned in a plate of soup. Now me, I dined here one evening. I noticed the way the soup was served. It was served from a tureen on the side table. Therefore, if anyone found a ring in their soup plate it could only have been placed there *either* by the person who was serving the soup (in this case Geronimo) or by the person whose soup plate it was. *You!* I do not think it was Geronimo. I think that *you* staged the return of the ring in the soup in that way because it amused you. You have, if I may make the criticism, rather too humorous a sense of the dramatic. To hold up the ring! To exclaim! I think you indulged your sense of humour there, mademoiselle, and did not realise that you betrayed yourself in so doing.'

'Is that all?' Valerie spoke scornfully.

'Oh, no, it is by no means all. You see, when Celia confessed that evening to having been responsible for the thefts here, I noticed several small points. For instance, in speaking of this ring she said, "I didn't realise how valuable it was. As soon as I knew, I managed to return it." How did she know, Miss Valerie? Who told her how valuable the ring was? And then again in speaking of the cut scarf, little Miss Celia said something like, "That didn't matter. Valerie didn't mind . . ." Why did you not mind if a good quality silk scarf belonging to you was cut to shreds? I formed the impression then and there that the whole campaign of stealing things, of making herself out to be a kleptomaniac, and so attracting the attention of Colin McNabb, had been thought out for Celia by *someone else*. Someone with far more intelligence than Celia Austin had and with a good working knowledge of psychology. You told her the ring was valuable; you took it from her and arranged for its return. In the same way it was at your suggestion that she slashed a scarf of yours to pieces.'

'These are all theories,' said Valerie, 'and rather farfetched theories at that. The inspector has already suggested to me that I put Celia up to doing these tricks.'

'And what did you say to him?'

'I said it was nonsense,' said Valerie.

'And what do you say to me?'

Valerie looked at him searchingly for a moment or two. Then she gave a short laugh, stubbed out her cigarette, leaned back thrusting a cushion behind her back, and said:

'You're quite right. I put her up to it.'

'May I ask you why?'

Valerie said impatiently:

'Oh, sheer foolish good nature. Benevolent interfering. There Celia was, mooning about like a little ghost, yearning over Colin who never looked at her. It all seemed so *silly*. Colin's one of those conceited opinionated young men wrapped up in psychology and complexes and emotional blocks and all the rest of it, and I thought it would be really rather fun to egg him on and make a fool of him. Anyway I hated to see Celia look so miserable, so I got hold of her, gave her a talking-to, explained in outline the whole scheme, and urged her on to it. She was a bit nervous, I think, about it all, but rather thrilled at the same time. Then, of course, one of the first things the little idiot does is to find Pat's ring left in the bathroom and pinch that—a really valuable piece of jewellery about which there'd be a lot of hoo-ha and the police would be called in and the whole thing might take a serious turn. So I grabbed the ring off her, told her I'd return it somehow, and urged her in future to stick to costume jewellery and cosmetics and a little wilful damage to something of mine which wouldn't land her in trouble.'

Poirot drew a deep breath.

'That was exactly what I thought,' he said.

'I wish that I hadn't done it now,' said Valerie sombrely. 'But I really did mean well. That's an atrocious thing to say and just like Jean Tomlinson, but there it is.'

'And now,' said Poirot, 'we come to this business of Patricia's ring. Celia gave it to you. You were to find it somewhere and return it to Patricia. But *before* returning it to Patricia,' he paused. 'What happened?'

He watched her fingers nervously plaiting and unplaiting the end of a fringed scarf that she was wearing round her neck. He went on, in an even more persuasive voice:

'You were hard up, eh, was that it?'

Without looking up at him she gave a short nod of the head.

'I said I'd come clean,' she said and there was bitterness in her voice. 'The trouble with me is, Monsieur Poirot, I'm a gambler. That's one of the things that's born in you and you can't do anything much about it. I belong to a little club in Mayfair—oh, I shan't tell you just where—I don't want to be responsible for getting it raided by the police or anything of that kind. We'll just let it go at the fact that I belong to it. There's roulette there, baccarat, all the rest of it. I've taken a nasty series of losses one after the other. I had this ring of Pat's. I happened to be passing a shop where there was a zircon ring. I thought to myself, 'If this diamond was replaced with a white zircon Pat would never know the difference!' You never do look at a ring you know really well. If the diamond seems a bit duller than usual you just think it needs cleaning or something like that. All right, I had an impulse. I fell. I prised out the diamond and sold it. Replaced it with a zircon and that night I pretended to find it in my soup. That was a damn' silly thing to do, too, I agree. There! Now you know it all. But honestly, I never meant Celia to be blamed for that.'

'No, no, I understand.' Poirot nodded his head. 'It was just an opportunity that came your way. It seemed easy and you took it. But you made there a great mistake, mademoiselle.'

'I realise that,' said Valerie dryly. Then she broke out unhappily :

'But what the hell! Does that matter now? Oh, turn me in if you like. Tell Pat. Tell the inspector. Tell the world! But what *good* is it going to do? How's it going to help us with finding out who killed Celia?'

Poirot rose to his feet.

'One never knows,' he said, 'what may help and what may not. One has to clear out of the way so many things that do not matter and that confuse the issue. It was important for me to know who had inspired the little Celia to play the part she did. I know that now. As to the ring, I suggest that you go yourself to Miss Patricia Lane and that you tell her what you did and express the customary sentiments.'

Valerie made a grimace.

'I dare say that's pretty good advice on the whole,' she said. 'All right, I'll go to Pat and I'll eat humble pie. Pat's a very decent sort. I'll tell her that when I can afford it again I'll replace the diamond. Is that what you want, M. Poirot?'

'It is not what I want, it is what is advisable.'

The door opened suddenly and Mrs Hubbard came in.

She was breathing hard and the expression in her face made Valerie exclaim :

'What's the matter, Mum? What's happened?'

Mrs Hubbard dropped into a chair.

'It's Mrs Nicoletis.'

'Mrs Nick? What about her?'

'Oh, my dear. She's *dead*.'

'Dead?' Valerie's voice came harshly. 'How? When?'

'It seems she was picked up in the street last night— they took her to the police station. They thought she was —was—'

'Drunk? I suppose . . .'

'Yes—she *had* been drinking. But anyway—she died—'

'Poor old Mrs Nick,' said Valerie. There was a tremor in her husky voice.

Poirot said gently:

'You were fond of her, mademoiselle?'

'It's odd in a way—she could be a proper old devil—but yes—I was . . . When I first came here—three years ago, she wasn't nearly as—as temperamental as she became later. She was good company—amusing—warm-hearted. She's changed a lot in the last year—'

Valerie looked at Mrs Hubbard.

'I suppose that's because she'd taken to drinking on the quiet—they found a lot of bottles and things in her room, didn't they?'

'Yes,' Mrs Hubbard hesitated, then burst out: 'I do blame myself—letting her go off home alone last night— she was afraid of something, you know.'

'Afraid?'

Poirot and Valerie said it in unison.

Mrs Hubbard nodded unhappily. Her mild round face was troubled.

'Yes. She kept saying she wasn't safe. I asked her to tell me what she was afraid of—and she snubbed me. And one never knew with her, of course, how much was exaggeration. But now—I wonder—'

Valerie said:

'You don't think that she—that she, too—that she was—'

She broke off with a look of horror in her eyes.

Poirot asked:

'What did they say was the cause of death?'

Mrs Hubbard said unhappily:

'They—they didn't say. There's to be an inquest—on Tuesday—'

CHAPTER FIFTEEN

In a quiet room at New Scotland Yard, four men were sitting round a table.

Presiding over the conference was Superintendent Wilding of the Narcotics squad. Next to him was Sergeant Bell, a young man of great energy and optimism who looked rather like an eager greyhound. Leaning back in his chair, quiet and alert, was Inspector Sharpe. The fourth man was Hercule Poirot. On the table was a rucksack.

Superintendent Wilding stroked his chin thoughtfully.

'It's an interesting idea, M. Poirot,' he said cautiously. 'Yes, it's an interesting idea.'

'It is, as I say, simply an idea,' said Poirot.

Wilding nodded.

'We've outlined the general position,' he said. 'Smuggling goes on all the time, of course, in one form or another. We clear up one lot of operators, and after a due interval things start again somewhere else. Speaking for my own branch, there's been a good lot of the stuff coming into this country in the last year and a half. Heroin mostly —a fair amount of coke. There are various depots dotted here and there on the Continent. The French police have got a lead or two as to how it comes into France—they're less certain how it goes out again.'

'Would I be right in saying,' Poirot asked, 'that your problem could be divided roughly under three heads. There is the problem of distribution, there is the problem of how the consignments enter the country, and there is the problem of who really runs the business and takes the main profits?'

'Roughly I'd say that's quite right. We know a fair amount about the small distributors and how the stuff is distributed. Some of the distributors we pull in, some we leave alone hoping that they may lead us to the big fish. It's distributed in a lot of different ways, night-clubs, pubs, drug stores, an odd doctor or so, fashionable women's dressmakers and hairdressers. It is handed over on race-courses, and in antique dealers', sometimes in a crowded multiple store. But I needn't tell you all this. It's not that side of it that's important. We can keep pace with all that fairly well. And we've got certain very shrewd suspicions as to what I've called the big fish. One or two very respect-able wealthy gentlemen against whom there's never a breath of suspicion. Very careful they are; they never handle the stuff themselves, and the little fry don't even know who they are. But every now and again, one of them makes a slip—and then—we get him.'

'That is all very much as I supposed. The line in which I am interested is the third line—how do the consignments come into the country?'

'Ah. We're an island. The most usual way is the good old-fashioned way of the sea. Running a cargo. Quiet landing somewhere on the east coast, or a little cove down south, by a motor-boat that's slipped quietly across the Channel. That succeeds for a bit but sooner or later we get a line on the particular fellow who owns the boat and once he's under suspicion his opportunity's gone. Once or twice lately the stuff's come in on one of the air liners. There's big money offered, and occasionally one of the stewards or one of the crew proves to be only too human. And then there are the commercial importers. Respectable firms that import grand pianos or what have you! They have quite a good run for a bit, but we usually get wise to them in the end.'

'You would agree that it is one of the chief difficulties when you are running an illicit trade—the entry from abroad into this country?'

'Decidedly. And I'll say more. For some time now, we've been worried. More stuff is coming in than we can keep pace with.'

'And what about other things, such as gems?'

Sergeant Bell spoke.

'There's a good deal of it going on, sir. Illicit diamonds

and other stones are coming out of South Africa and Australia, some from the Far East. They're coming into this country in a steady stream, and we don't know how. The other day a young woman, an ordinary tourist, in France, was asked by a casual acquaintance if she'd take a pair of shoes across the Channel. Not new ones, nothing dutiable, just some shoes someone had left behind. She agreed quite unsuspiciously. We happened to be on to that. The heels of the shoes turned out to be hollow and packed with uncut diamonds.'

Superintendent Wilding said:

'But look here, M. Poirot, what is it you're on the track of, dope or smuggled gems?'

'Either. Anything, in fact, of high value and small bulk. There is an opening, it seems to me, for what you might call a freight service, conveying goods such as I have described to and fro across the Channel. Stolen jewellery, the stones removed from their settings, could be taken out of England, illicit stones and drugs brought in. It could be a small independent agency, unconnected with distribution, that carried stuff on a commission basis. And the profits might be high.'

'I'll say you're right there! You can pack ten or twenty thousand pounds' worth of heroin in a very small space and the same goes for uncut stones of high quality.'

'You see,' said Poirot, 'the weakness of the smuggler is always the human element. Sooner or later you suspect a *person*, an air line steward, a yachting enthusiast with a small cabin cruiser, the woman who travels to and fro to France too often, the importer who seems to be making more money than is reasonable, the man who lives well without visible means of support. But if the stuff is brought into this country by an innocent person, and what is more, *by a different person each time*, then the difficulties of spotting the cargoes are enormously increased.'

Wilding pushed a finger towards the rucksack. 'And that's your suggestion?'

'Yes. Who is the person who is least vulnerable to suspicion these days? The student. The earnest, hard-working student. Badly off, travelling about with no more luggage than what he can carry on his back. Hitch-hiking his way across Europe. If one particular student were to bring the stuff in all the time, no doubt you'd get wise to him or her, but the whole essence of the arrangement is that the carriers are innocent and that there are a lot of them.'

Wilding rubbed his jaw.

'Just how exactly do you think it's managed, M. Poirot?' he asked.

Hercule Poirot shrugged his shoulders.

'As to that it is my guess only. No doubt I am wrong in many details, but I should say that it worked roughly like this: First, a line of rucksacks is placed on the market. They are of the ordinary, conventional type, just like any other rucksack, well and strongly made and suitable for their purpose. When I say "just like any other rucksack" that is not so. The lining at the base is slightly different. As you see, it is quite easily removable and is of a thick-ness and composition to allow of rouleaux of gems or powder concealed in the corrugations. You would never suspect it unless you were looking for it. Pure heroin or pure cocaine would take up very little room.'

'Too true,' said Wilding. 'Why,' he measured with rapid fingers, 'you could bring in stuff worth five or six thousand pounds each time without anyone being the wiser.'

'Exactly,' said Hercule Poirot. '*Alors!* The rucksacks are made, put on the market, are on sale—probably in more than one shop. The proprietor of the shop may be in the racket or he may not. It may be that he has just been sold a cheap line which he finds profitable, since his prices will compare favourably with that charged by other camp-ing outfit sellers. There is, of course, a definite organisation in the background; a carefully kept list of students at the medical schools, at London University and at other places. Someone who is himself a student, or posing as a student, is probably at the head of the racket. Students go abroad. At some point in the return journey a duplicate rucksack is exchanged. The student returns to England; customs investigations will be perfunctory. The student arrives back at his or her hostel, unpacks, and the empty rucksack is tossed into a cupboard or into a corner of the room. At this point there will be again an exchange of rucksacks or possibly the false bottom will be neatly extracted and an innocent one replace it.'

'And you think that's what happened at Hickory Road?'

Poirot nodded.

'That is my suspicion. Yes.'

'But what put you on to it, M. Poirot—assuming you're right, that is?'

'A rucksack was cut to pieces,' said Poirot. 'Why? Since the reason is not plain, one has to imagine a reason. There is something queer about the rucksacks that come to Hickory Road. They are too cheap. There have been a series of peculiar happenings at Hickory Road, but the girl responsible for them swore that the destruction of the rucksack was *not* her doing. Since she has confessed to the other things why should she deny that, unless she was speaking the truth? So there must be another reason for the destruction of the rucksack—and to destroy a rucksack, I may say, is not an easy thing. It was hard work and someone must have been pretty desperate to undertake it. I got my clue when I found that roughly—(only roughly, alas, because people's memories after a period of some months are not too certain) but roughly—that that rucksack was destroyed at about the date when a police officer called to see the person in charge of the hostel. The actual reason that the police officer called had to do with quite another matter, but I will put it to you like this: You are someone concerned in this smuggling racket. You go home to the house that evening and you are informed that the police have called and are at the moment upstairs with Mrs Hubbard. Immediately you assume that the police are on to the smuggling racket, that they have come to make an investigation; and let us say that at that moment *there is in the house a rucksack* just brought back from abroad containing— or which has recently contained

—contraband. Now, if the police have a line on what has been going on, they will have come to Hickory Road for the express purpose of examining the rucksacks of the students. You dare not walk out of the house with the rucksack in question because, for all you know, somebody may have been left outside by the police to watch the house with just that object in view, and a rucksack is not an easy thing to conceal or disguise. The only thing you can think of is to rip up the rucksack, and cram the pieces away among the junk in the boiler-house. If there is dope or gems on the premises, they can be concealed in bath salts as a temporary measure. But even an empty rucksack, if it had held dope, might yield traces of heroin or cocaine on close examination or analysis. So the rucksack must be destroyed. You agree that that is possible?'

'It's an idea, as I said before,' said Superintendent Wilding.

'It also seems possible that a small incident not hitherto regarded as important may be connected with the rucksack. According to the Italian servant, Geronimo, on the day, or one of the days, when the police called, the light in the hall had gone. He went to look for a bulb to replace it; found the spare bulbs, too, were missing. He was quite sure that a day or two previously there had been spare bulbs in the drawer. It seems to me a possibility—this is far-fetched and I would not say that I am sure of it, you understand, it is a mere possibility—that there was someone with a guilty conscience who had been mixed up with a smuggling racket before and who feared that his face might be known to the police if they saw him in a bright light. So he quietly removed the bulb from the hall light and took away the new ones so that it should not be replaced. As a result the hall was illuminated by a candle only. This, as I say, is merely a supposition.'

'It's an ingenious idea,' said Wilding.

'It's possible, sir,' said Sergeant Bell eagerly. 'The more I think of it the more possible I think it is.'

'But if so,' went on Wilding, 'there's more to it than just Hickory Road?'

Poirot nodded.

'Oh yes. The organisation must cover a wide range of students' clubs and so on.'

'You have to find a connecting link between them,' said Wilding.

Inspector Sharpe spoke for the first time.

'There is such a link, sir,' he said, 'or there was. A woman who ran several student clubs and organisations. A woman who was right on the spot at Hickory Road. Mrs Nicoletis.'

Wilding flicked a quick glance at Poirot.

'Yes,' said Poirot. 'Mrs Nicoletis fits the bill. She had a financial interest in all these places though she didn't run them herself. Her method was to get someone of unimpeachable integrity and antecedents to run the place. My friend Mrs Hubbard is such a person. The financial backing was supplied by Mrs Nicoletis—but there again I suspect her of being only a figurehead.'

'H'm,' said Wilding. 'I think it would be interesting to know a little more about Mrs Nicoletis.'

Sharpe nodded.

'We're investigating her,' he said. 'Her background and where she came from. It has to be done carefully. We don't want to alarm our birds too soon. We're looking into her financial background, too. My word, that woman was a tartar if there ever was one.'

He described his experiences of Mrs Nicoletis when confronted with a search warrant.

'Brandy bottles, eh?' said Wilding. 'So she drank? Well, that ought to make it easier. What's happened to her? Hooked it—?'

'No sir. She's dead.'

'Dead?' Wilding raised his eyebrows. 'Monkey business, do you mean?'

'We think so—yes. We'll know for certain after the autopsy. I think myself she'd begun to crack. Maybe she didn't bargain for murder.'

'You're talking about the Celia Austin case. Did the girl know something?'

'She knew something,' said Poirot, 'but if I may so put it, I do not think she knew what it was she knew!'

'You mean she knew something but didn't appreciate the implications of it?'

'Yes. Just that. She was not a clever girl. She would be quite likely to fail to grasp an inference. But having seen something, or heard something, she may have mentioned the fact quite unsuspiciously.'

'You've no idea what she saw or heard, M. Poirot?'

'I make guesses,' said Poirot. 'I cannot do more. There has been mention of a passport. Did someone in the house have a false passport allowing them to go to and fro to the Continent under another name? Would the revelation of that fact be a serious danger to that person? Did she see the rucksack being tampered with or did she, perhaps, one day see someone removing the false bottom from the ruck-sack without realising what it was that that person was doing? Did she perhaps see the person who removed the light bulbs? And mention the fact to him or her, not realising that it was of any importance? Ah, *mon dieu*!' said Hercule Poirot with irritation. 'Guesses! guesses! guesses! One must *know* more. Always one must know more!'

'Well,' said Sharpe, 'we can make a start on Mrs Nicoletis's antecedents. Something may come up.'

'She was put out of the way because they thought she might talk? Would she have talked?'

'She'd been drinking secretly for some time . . . and that means her nerves were shot to pieces,' said Sharpe. 'She might have broken down and spilled the whole thing. Turned Queen's Evidence.'

'She didn't really run the racket, I suppose?'

Poirot shook his head.

'I should not think so, no. She was out in the open, you see. She knew what was going on, of course, but I should not say she was the brains behind it. No.'

'Any idea who is the brains behind it?'

'I could make a guess—I might be wrong. Yes—I *might* be wrong!'

CHAPTER SIXTEEN

'Hickory, dickory, dock,' said Nigel, 'the mouse ran up the clock. The police said "Boo," I wonder who, will eventually stand in the Dock?'

He added:

'To tell or not to tell? *That* is the question!'

He poured himself out a fresh cup of coffee and brought it back to the breakfast table.

'Tell what?' asked Len Bateson.

'Anything one knows,' said Nigel, with an airy wave of the hand.

Jean Tomlinson said disapprovingly:

'But of course! If we have any information that may be of use, of course we must tell the police. That would be only right.'

'And there speaks our bonnie Jean,' said Nigel.

'*Moi je n'aime pas les flics,*' said René offering his contribution to the discussion.

'Tell what?' Leonard Bateson asked again.

'The things we know,' said Nigel. 'About each other, I mean,' he added helpfully. His glance swept round the breakfast-table with a malicious gleam.

'After all,' he said cheerfully, 'we all *do* know lots of things about each other, don't we? I mean, one's bound to, living in the same house.'

'But who is to decide what is important or not? There are many things no business of the police at all,' said Mr Achmed Ali. He spoke hotly, with an injured remembrance of the inspector's sharp remarks about his collection of postcards.

'I hear,' said Nigel, turning towards Mr Akibombo, 'that they found some very interesting things in *your* room.'

Owing to his colour, Mr Akibombo was not able to blush, but his eyelids blinked in a discomfited manner.

'Very much superstition in my country,' he said. 'My grandfather give me things to bring here. I keep out of feeling of piety and respect. I, myself, am modern and scientific; not believe in voodoo, but owing to imperfect command of language I find very difficult to explain to policeman.'

'Even dear little Jean has her secrets, I expect,' said Nigel, turning his gaze back to Miss Tomlinson.

Jean said hotly that she wasn't going to be insulted.

'I shall leave this place and go to the Y.W.C.A.,' she said.

'Come now, Jean,' said Nigel. 'Give us another chance.'

'Oh, cut it out, Nigel!' said Valerie wearily. 'The police have to snoop, I suppose, under the circumstances.'

Colin McNabb cleared his throat, preparatory to making a remark.

'In my opinion,' he said judicially, 'the present position ought to be made clear to us. What exactly was the cause of Mrs Nick's death?'

'We'll hear at the inquest, I suppose,' said Valerie, impatiently.

'I very much doubt it,' said Colin. 'In my opinion they'll adjourn the inquest.'

'I suppose it was her heart, wasn't it?' said Patricia. 'She fell down in the street.'

'Drunk and incapable,' said Len Bateson. 'That's how she got taken to the police station.'

'So she *did* drink,' said Jean. 'You know, I always thought so. When the police searched the house they found cupboards full of empty brandy bottles in her room, I believe,' she added.

'Trust our Jean to know all the dirt,' said Nigel approvingly.

'Well, that does explain why she was sometimes so odd in her manner,' said Patricia.

Colin cleared his throat again.

'Ahem!' he said. 'I happened to observe her going into The Queen's Necklace on Saturday evening, when I was on my way home.'

'That's where she got tanked up, I suppose,' said Nigel.

'I suppose she just died of drink, then?' said Jean.

Len Bateson shook his head.

'Cerebral hæmorrhage?' I rather doubt it.'

'For goodness' sake, you don't think *she* was murdered too, do you?' said Jean.

'I bet she was,' said Sally Finch. 'Nothing would surprise me less.'

'Please,' said Mr Akibombo. 'It is thought someone killed her? Is that right?'

He looked from face to face.

'We've no reason to suppose anything of the sort yet,' said Colin.

'But who would want to kill her?' demanded Genevieve. 'Had she much money to leave? If she was rich it is possible, I suppose.'

'She was a maddening woman, my dear,' said Nigel. 'I'm sure everybody wanted to kill her. I often did,' he added, helping himself happily to marmalade.

II

'Please, Miss Sally, may I ask you a question? It is after what was said at breakfast. I have been thinking very much.'

'Well, I shouldn't think too much if I were you, Akibombo,' said Sally. 'It isn't healthy.'

Sally and Akibombo were partaking of an open-air lunch in Regent's Park. Summer was officially supposed to have come and the restaurant was open.

'All this morning,' said Akibombo mournfully, 'I have been much disturbed. I cannot answer my professor's questions good at all. He is not pleased at me. He says to me that I copy large bits out of books and do not think for myself. But I am here to acquire wisdom from much books and it seems to me that they say better in the books than the way I put it, because I have not good command of the English. And besides, this morning I find it very hard to think at all except of what goes on at Hickory Road and difficulties there.'

'I'll say you're right about that,' said Sally. 'I just couldn't' concentrate myself this morning.'

'So that is why I ask you please to tell me certain things, because as I say, I have been thinking very much.'

'Well, let's hear what you've been thinking about, then.'

'Well, it is this borr—ass—sic.'

'Borr-ass-sic? Oh, boracic! Yes. What about it?'

'Well, I do not understand very well. It is an acid, they say? An acid like sulphuric acid?'

'Not like sulphuric acid, no,' said Sally.

'It is not something for laboratory experiment only?'

'I shouldn't imagine they ever did any experiments in laboratories with it. It's something quite mild and harmless.'

'You mean, even you could put it in your *eyes*?'

'That's right. That's just what one does use it for.'

'Ah, that explains that then. Mr Chandra Lal, he have little white bottle with white powder, and he puts powder in hot water and bathes his eyes with it. He keeps it in bathroom and then it is not there one day and he is very angry. That would be the bor-ac-ic, yes?'

'What *is* all this about boracic?'

'I tell you by and by. Please not now. I think some more.'

'Well, don't go sticking your neck out,' said Sally. 'I don't want yours to be the next corpse, Akibombo.'

III

'Valerie, do you think you could give me some advice?'

'Of course I could give you advice, Jean, though I don't know why anyone ever wants advice. They never take it.'

'It's really a matter of conscience,' said Jean.

'Then I'm the last person you ought to ask. I haven't got any conscience, to speak of.'

'Oh, Valerie, don't say things like that!'

'Well, it's quite true,' said Valerie. She stubbed out a cigarette as she spoke. 'I smuggle clothes in from Paris and tell the most frightful lies about their faces to the hideous women who come to the *salon*. I even travel on buses without paying my fare when I'm hard up. But come on, tell me. What's it all about?'

'It's what Nigel said at breakfast. If one knows something about someone else, do you think one ought to tell?'

'What an idiotic question! You can't put a thing like that in general terms. What is it you want to tell, or don't want to tell?'

'It's about a passport.'

'A passport?' Valerie sat up, surprised. 'Whose passport?'

'Nigel's. He's got a false passport.'

'Nigel?' Valerie sounded disbelieving. 'I don't believe it. It seems most improbable.'

'But he has. And you know, Valerie, I believe there's some question—I think I heard the police saying that Celia had said something about a passport. Supposing she'd found out about it and he killed her?'

'Sounds very melodramatic,' said Valerie. 'But frankly, I don't believe a word of it. What is this story about a passport?'

'I saw it.'

'How did you see it?'

'Well, it was absolutely an accident,' said Jean. 'I was looking for something in my despatch case a week or two ago, and by mistake I must have looked in Nigel's attaché-case instead. They were both on the shelf in the common-room.'

Valerie laughed rather disagreeably.

'Tell that to the marines!' she said. 'What were you really doing? Snooping?'

'No, of course not!' Jean sounded justly indignant. 'The one thing I'd never do is to look among anybody's private papers. I'm not that sort of person. It was just that I was feeling rather absent-minded, so I opened the case and I was just sorting through it . . .'

'Look here, Jean, you can't get away with that. Nigel's attaché-case is a good deal larger than yours and it's an entirely different colour. While you're admitting things you might just as well admit that you *are* that sort of person. All right. You found a chance to go through some of Nigel's things and you took it.'

Jean rose.

'Of course, Valerie, if you're going to be so unpleasant and so very unfair and unkind, I shall . . .'

'Oh, come back, child!' said Valerie. 'Get on with it. I'm getting interested now. I want to know.'

'Well, there was this passport,' said Jean. 'It was down at the bottom and it had a name on it. Stanford or Stanley or some name like that, and I thought, "How odd that Nigel should have somebody else's passport here." I opened it and the photograph inside was Nigel! So don't you see, he must be leading a double life? What I wonder is, ought I to tell the police? Do you think it's my duty?'

Valerie laughed.

'Bad luck, Jean,' she said. 'As a matter of fact, I believe there's a quite simple explanation. Pat told me. Nigel came into some money, or something, on condition that he changed his name. He did it perfectly properly by deed poll or whatever it is, but that's all it is. I believe his original name *was* Stanfield or Stanley, or something like that.'

'Oh!' Jean looked thoroughly chagrined.

'Ask Pat about it if you don't believe me,' said Valerie.

'Oh—no—well, if it's as you say, I must have made a mistake.'

'Better luck next time,' said Valerie.

'I don't know what you mean, Valerie.'

'You'd like to get your knife into Nigel, wouldn't you? And get him in wrong with the police?'

Jean drew herself up.

'You may not believe me, Valerie,' she said, 'but all I wanted to do was my duty.'

She left the room.

'Oh, hell!' said Valerie.

There was a tap at the door and Sally entered.

'What's the matter, Valerie? You're looking a bit down in the mouth.'

'It's that disgusting Jean. She really is *too* awful! You don't think, do you, that there's the remotest chance it was Jean that bumped off poor Celia? I should rejoice madly if I ever saw Jean in the dock.'

'I'm with you there,' said Sally. 'But I don't think it's particularly likely. I don't think Jean would ever stick her neck out enough to murder anybody.'

'What do you think about Mrs Nick?'

'I just don't know what to think. I suppose we shall hear soon.'

'I'd say ten to one she was bumped off, too,' said Valerie.

'But why? What's going on here?' said Sally.

'I wish I knew. Sally do you ever find yourself looking at people?'

'What do you mean, Val, looking at people?'

'Well, looking and wondering, "Is it *you*?" I've got a feeling, Sally, that there's someone here who's mad. *Really* mad. Bad mad, I mean—not just thinking they're a cucumber.'

'That may well be,' said Sally. She shivered.

'Ouch!' she said. 'Somebody's walking over my grave.'

IV

'Nigel I've got something I *must* tell you.'

'Well, what is it, Pat? Nigel was burrowing frantically in his chest of drawers. 'What the hell I did with those notes of mine I can't imagine. I shoved them in here, I thought.'

'Oh, Nigel, don't scrabble like that! You leave everything in such a frightful mess and I've just tidied it.'

'Well, what the hell, I've got to find my notes, haven't I?'

'Nigel, you *must* listen!'

'O.K., Pat, don't look so desperate. What is it?'

'It's something I've got to confess.'

'Not murder, I hope?' said Nigel, with his usual flippancy.

'No, of course not!'

'Good. Well, what lesser sin?'

'It was one day when I mended your socks and I brought them along here to your room and was putting them away in your drawer . . .'

'Yes?'

'And the bottle of morphia was there. The one you told me about, that you got from the hospital.'

'Yes, and you made such a fuss about it!'

'But, Nigel it was there in your drawer among your socks, where *anybody* could have found it.'

'Why should they? Nobody else goes routing about among my socks except you.'

'Well, it seemed to me dreadful to leave it about like that, and I know you'd said you were going to get rid of it after you'd won your bet, but in the meantime there it was, still there.'

'Of course. I hadn't got the third thing yet.'

'Well, I thought it was very wrong, and so I took the bottle out of the drawer and I emptied the poison out of it, and I replaced it with some ordinary bicarbonate of soda. It looked almost exactly the same.'

Nigel paused in his scramble for his lost notes.

'Good lord!' he said. 'Did you really? You mean that when I was swearing to Len and old Colin that the stuff was morphine sulphate or tartrate or whatever it was, it was merely bicarbonate of soda all the time?'

'Yes. You see . . .'

Nigel interrupted her. He was frowning.

'I'm not sure, you know, that that doesn't invalidate the bet. Of course, *I'd* no idea—'

'But Nigel, it was really *dangerous* keeping it there.'

'Oh, lord, Pat, must you always fuss so? What did you do with the actual stuff?'

'I put it in the soda bic bottle and I hid it at the back of my handkerchief drawer.'

Nigel looked at her in mild surprise.

'Really, Pat, your logical thought processes beggar description! What was the point?'

'I felt it was safer there.'

'My dear girl, either the morphia should have been under lock and key, or if it wasn't, it couldn't really matter whether it was among my socks or your handkerchiefs.'

'Well, it did matter. For one thing, I have a room to

myself and you share yours.'

'Why, you don't think poor old Len was going to pinch the morphia off me, do you?'

'I wasn't going to tell you about it, ever, but I must now. Because, you see, it's *gone*.'

'You mean the police have swiped it?'

'No. It disappeared before that.'

'Do you mean . . .?' Nigel gazed at her in consternation. 'Let's get this straight. There's a bottle labelled "Soda Bic," containing morphine sulphate, which is knocking about the place somewhere, and at any time someone may take a heaping teaspoonful of it if they've got a pain in their middle? Good God, Pat! You *have* done it! Why the hell didn't you throw the stuff away if you were so upset about it?'

'Because I thought it was valuable and ought to go back to the hospital instead of being just thrown away. As soon as you'd won your bet, I meant to give it to Celia and ask her to put it back.'

'You're sure you *didn't* give it to her?'

'No, of course not. You mean I gave it to her, and she took it and it *was* suicide, and it was all my fault?'

'Calm down. When did it disappear?'

'I don't know exactly. I looked for it the day before Celia died. I couldn't find it, but I just thought I'd perhaps put it somewhere else.'

'It was gone the day *before* she died?'

'I suppose,' said Patricia, her face white, 'that I've been very stupid.'

'That's putting it mildly,' said Nigel. 'To what lengths can a muddled mind and an active conscience go!'

'Nigel. D'you think I ought to tell the police?'

'Oh, hell!' said Nigel. 'I suppose so, yes. And it's going to be all my fault.'

'Oh, no, Nigel darling, it's me. I—'

'I pinched the damned stuff in the first place,' said Nigel. 'It all seemed to be a very amusing stunt at the time. But now—I can already hear the vitriolic remarks from the bench.'

'I *am* sorry. When I took it I really meant it for—'

'You meant it for the best. *I* know. I know! Look here, Pat, I simply can't believe the stuff has disappeared. You've forgotten just where you put it. You do mislay things sometimes, you know.'

'Yes, but—'

She hesitated, a shade of doubt appearing on her frowning face.

Nigel rose briskly.

'Let's go along to your room and have a thorough search.'

V

'Nigel, those are my *underclothes*.'

'Really, Pat, you can't go all prudish on me at this stage. Down among the panties is just where you would hide a bottle, now, isn't it?'

'Yes, but I'm sure I—'

'We can't be sure of anything until we've looked everywhere. And I'm jolly well going to do it.'

There was a perfunctory tap on the door and Sally Finch entered. Her eyes widened with surprise. Pat, clasping a handful of Nigel's socks, was sitting on the bed, and Nigel, the bureau drawers all pulled out, was burrowing like an excited terrier into a heap of pullovers whilst about him were strewn panties, brassières, stockings, and other component parts of female attire.

'For land's sake,' said Sally, 'what goes on?'

'Looking for bicarbonate,' said Nigel briefly.

'Bicarbonate? Why?'

'I've got a pain,' said Nigel, grinning. 'A pain in my tum-tum-tum—and nothing but bicarbonate will assuage it.'

'I've got some somewhere, I believe.'

'No good, Sally, it's got to be Pat's. Hers is the only brand that will ease my particular ailment.'

'You're crazy,' said Sally. 'What's he up to, Pat?'

Patricia shook her head miserably.

'*You* haven't seen my soda bic, have you, Sally?' she

asked. 'Just a little in the bottom of the bottle.'

'No.' Sally looked at her curiously. Then she frowned. 'Let me see. Somebody around here—no, I can't remember— Have you got a stamp, Pat? I want to mail a letter and I've run out.'

'In the drawer there.'

Sally opened the shallow drawer of the writing-table, took out a book of stamps, extracted one, affixed it to the letter she held in her hand, dropped the stamp book back in the drawer, and put twopence halfpenny on the desk.

'Thanks. Shall I mail this letter of yours at the same time?'

'Yes—no—no, I think I'll wait.'

Sally nodded and left the room.

Pat dropped the socks she had been holding, and twisted her fingers nervously together.

'Nigel?'

'Yes?' Nigel had transferred his attention to the wardrobe and was looking in the pockets of a coat.

'There's something else I've got to confess.'

'Good lord, Pat, what else have you been doing?'

'I'm afraid you'll be angry.'

'I'm past being angry. I'm just plain scared. If Celia was poisoned with the stuff that I pinched, I shall probably go to prison for years and years, even if they don't hang me.'

'It's nothing to do with that. It's about your father.'

'What?' Nigel spun round, an expression of incredulous astonishment on his face.

'You do know he's very ill, don't you?'

'I don't care how ill he is.'

'It said so on the wireless last night. "Sir Arthur Stanley, the famous research chemist, is lying in a very critical condition." '

'So nice to be a V.I.P. All the world gets the news when you're ill.'

'Nigel, if he's dying, you ought to be reconciled to him.'

'Like hell, I will!'

'But if he's dying.'

'He's the same swine dying as he was when he was in the

pink of condition!'

'You mustn't be like that, Nigel. So bitter and unforgiving.'

'Listen, Pat—I told you once: he killed my mother.'

'I know you said so, and I know you adored her. But I do think, Nigel, that you sometimes *exaggerate*. Lots of husbands are unkind and unfeeling and their wives resent it and it makes them very unhappy. But to say your father killed your mother is an extravagant statement and isn't really true.'

'You know so much about it, don't you?'

'I know that some day you'll regret not having made it up with your father before he died. That's why—' Pat paused and braced herself. 'That's why I—I've written to your father—telling him—'

'You've written to him? Is that the letter Sally wanted to post?' He strode over to the writing-table. '*I* see.'

He picked up the letter lying addressed and stamped, and with quick nervous fingers, he tore it into small pieces and threw it into the waste-paper basket.

'That's that! And don't you dare do anything of that kind again.'

'Really, Nigel, you are absolutely childish. You can tear the letter up, but you can't stop me writing another, and I shall.'

'You're so incurably sentimental. Did it never occur to you that when I said my father killed my mother, I was stating just a plain unvarnished *fact*. My mother died of an overdose of medinal. Took it by mistake, they said at the inquest. *But she didn't take it by mistake*. It was given to her, deliberately, by my father. He wanted to marry another woman, you see, and my mother wouldn't give him a divorce. It's a plain sordid murder story. What would you have done in my place? Denounced him to the police? My mother wouldn't have wanted that . . . So I did the only thing I could do—told the swine I knew—and cleared out—for ever. I even changed my name.'

'Nigel—I'm sorry . . . I never dreamed . . .'

'Well, you know now . . . The respected and famous

Arthur Stanley with his reseaches and his antibiotics. Flourishing like the green bay tree! But his fancy piece didn't marry him after all. She sheered off. I think she guessed what he'd done—'

'Nigel dear, how awful—I am sorry . . .'

'All right. We won't talk of it again. Let's get back to this blasted bicarbonate business. Now think back carefully to exactly what you did with the stuff. Put your head in your hands and *think*, Pat.'

VI

Genevieve entered the common-room in a state of great excitement. She spoke to the assembled students in a low thrilled voice.

'I am sure now, but absolutely sure I know who killed the little Celia.'

'Who was it, Genevieve?' demanded René. 'What has arrived to make you so positive?'

Genevieve looked cautiously round to make sure the door of the common-room was closed. She lowered her voice.

'It is Nigel Chapman.'

'Nigel Chapman, but why?'

'Listen. I pass along the corridor to go down the stairs just now and I hear voices in Patricia's room. It is Nigel who speaks.'

'Nigel? In Patricia's room?' Jean spoke in a disapproving voice. But Genevieve swept on.

'And he is saying to her that his father killed his mother and that, *pour ça*, he has changed his name. So it is clear is it not? His father was a convicted murderer, and Nigel he has the hereditary taint . . .'

'It is possible,' said Mr Chandra Lal, dwelling pleasurably on the possibility. 'It is certainly possible. He is so violent, Nigel, so unbalanced. No self-control. You agree? He turned condescendingly to Akibombo, who nodded an enthusiastic black woolly head and showed his whit teeth in a pleased smile.

'I've always felt very strongly,' said Jean, 'that Nigel has *no* moral sense . . . A thoroughly *degenerate* character.'

'It is sex murder, yes,' said Mr Achmed Ali. 'He sleeps with this girl, then he kills her. Because she is nice girl, respectable, she will expect marriage. . . .'

'Rot,' said Leonard Bateson explosively.

'What did you say?'

'I said ROT!' roared Len.

CHAPTER SEVENTEEN

Seated in a room at the police station, Nigel looked nervously into the stern eyes of Inspector Sharpe. Stammering slightly, he had just brought his narrative to a close.

'You realise. Mr Chapman, that what you have just told us is very serious? Very serious indeed.'

'Of course I realise it. I wouldn't have come here to tell you about it unless I'd felt that it was urgent.'

'And you say Miss Lane can't remember exactly when she last saw this bicarbonate bottle containing morphine?'

'She's got herself all muddled up. The more she tries to think the more uncertain she gets. She said I flustered her. She's trying to think it out while I came round to you.'

'We'd better go round to Hickory Road right away.'

As the inspector spoke the telephone on the table rang, and the constable who had been taking notes of Nigel's story stretched out his hand and lifted the receiver.

'It's Miss Lane now,' he said, as he listened. 'Wanting to speak to Mr Chapman.'

Nigel leaned across the table and took the receiver from him.

'Pat? Nigel here.'

The girl's voice came, breathless, eager, the words tumbling over each other.

'Nigel. *I think I've got it!* I mean, I think I know now who must have taken—you know—taken it from my handkerchief drawer, I mean—you see, there's only one person who—'

The voice broke off.

'Pat. Hallo? Are you there? Who was it?'

'I can't tell you now. Later. You'll be coming round?'

The receiver was near enough for the constable and the inspector to have heard the conversation clearly, and the latter nodded in answer to Nigel's questioning look.

'Tell her "at once," ' he said.

'We're coming round at once,' said Nigel. 'On our way this minute.'

'Oh! Good. I'll be in my room.'

'So long, Pat.'

Hardly a word was spoken during the brief ride to Hickory Road. Sharpe wondered to himself whether this was a break at last. Would Patricia Lane have any definite evidence to offer, or would it be pure surmise on her part? Clearly she had remembered *something* that had seemed to her important. He supposed that she had been telephoning from the hall, and that therefore she had had to be guarded in her language. At this time in the evening so many people would have been passing through.

Nigel opened the front door at 26 Hickory Road with his key and they passed inside. Through the open door of the common-room, Sharpe could see the rumpled red head of Leonard Bateson bent over some books.

Nigel led the way upstairs and along the passage to Pat's room. He gave a short tap on the door and entered.

'Hallo, Pat. Here we—'

His voice stopped, dying away in a long choking gasp. He stood motionless. Over his shoulder, Sharpe saw also what there was to see.

Patricia Lane lay slumped on the floor.

The inspector pushed Nigel gently aside. He went forward and knelt down by the girl's huddled body. He raised her head, felt for the pulse, then delicately let the head resume its former position. He rose to his feet, his face grim and set.

'No?' said Nigel, his voice high and unnatural. 'No. No. No.'

'Yes, Mr Chapman. She's dead.'

'No, *no*. Not Pat! Dear stupid Pat. How—'

'With this.'

It was a simple, quickly improvised weapon. A marble paperweight slipped into a woollen sock.

'Struck on the back of the head. A very efficacious weapon. If it's any consolation to you, Mr Chapman, I don't think she even knew what happened to her.[2]

Nigel sat down shakily on the bed. He said:

'That's one of *my* socks . . . She was going to mend it . . . Oh, God, she was going to mend it . . .'

Suddenly he began to cry. He cried like a child—with abandon and without self-consciousness.

Sharpe was continuing his reconstruction.

'It was someone she knew quite well. Someone who picked up a sock and just slipped the paperweight into it. Do you recognise the paperweight, Mr Chapman?'

He rolled the sock back so as to display it.

Nigel, still weeping, looked.

'Pat always had it on her desk. A Lion of Lucerne.[3]

He buried his face in his hands.

'Pat—oh, Pat! What shall I do without you!'

Suddenly he sat upright, flinging back his untidy fair hair.

'I'll kill whoever did this! I'll kill him! Murdering swine!'

'Gently, Mr Chapman. Yes, yes, I know how you feel. A brutal piece of work.'

'Pat never harmed anybody . . .'

Speaking soothingly, Inspector Sharpe got him out of the room. Then he went back himself into the bedroom. He stooped over the dead girl. Very gently he detached something from between her fingers.

II

Geronimo, perspiration running down his forehead, turned frightened dark eyes from one face to the other.

'I see nothing. I hear nothing, I tell you. I do not know anything *at all*. I am with Maria in kitchen. I put the Minestrone on, I grate the cheese—'

Sharpe interrupted the catalogue.

'Nobody's accusing you. We just want to get some times quite clear. Who was in and out of the house the last hour?'

'I do not know. How should I know?'

'But you can see very clearly from the kitchen window who goes in and out, can't you?'

'Perhaps, yes.'

'Then just tell us.'

'They come in and out all the time at this hour of the
day.'

'Who was in the house from six o'clock until six thirty-
five when we arrived?'

'Everybody except Mr Nigel and Mrs Hubbard and Miss
Hobhouse.'

'When did they go out?'

'Mrs Hubbard she go out before tea-time, she has not
come back yet.'

'Go on.'

'Mr Nigel goes out about half an hour ago, just before six
—look very upset. He come back with you just now—'

'That's right, yes.'

'Miss Valerie, she goes out just at six o'clock. Time signal,
pip, pip, pip. Dressed for cocktails, very smart. She still out.'

'And everybody else is here?'

'Yes, sir. All here.'

Sharpe looked down at his notebook. The time of Patricia's call was noted there. Eight minutes past six, exactly.

'Everybody else was here, in the house? Nobody came
back during that time?'

'Only Miss Sally. She been down to pillar-box with letter
and come back in—'

'Do you know what time she came in?'

Geronimo frowned.

'She came back while the news was going on.'

'After six, then?'

'Yes, sir.'

'What part of the news was it?'

'I don't remember, sir. But before the sport. Because when
sport come we switch off.'

Sharpe smiled grimly. It was a wide field. Only Nigel
Chapman, Valerie Hobhouse and Mrs Hubbard could be
excluded. It would mean long and exhaustive questioning.
Who had been in the common-room, who had left it? And
when? Who could vouch for who? Add to that, that many
of the students, especially the Asiatic and African ones,

were constitutionally vague about times, and the task was no enviable one.

But it would have to be done.

III

In Mrs Hubbard's room the atmosphere was unhappy. Mrs Hubbard herself, still in her outdoor things, her nice round face strained and anxious, sat on the sofa. Sharpe and Sergeant Cobb sat at a small table.

'I think she telephoned from in here,' said Sharpe. 'Around about 6.8 several people left or entered the common-room or so they say—and nobody saw or noticed or heard the hall telephone being used. Of course, their times aren't reliable, half these people never seem to look at a clock. But I think that anyway she'd come in here if she wanted to telephone the police station. You were out, Mrs Hubbard, but I don't suppose you lock your door?'

Mrs Hubbard shook her head.

'Mrs Nicoletis always did, but I never do—'

'Well then, Patricia Lane comes in here to telephone, all agog with what she's remembered. Then, whilst she was talking, the door opened and somebody looked in or came in. Patricia stalled and hung up. Was that because she recognised the intruder as the person whose name she was just about to say? Or was it just a general precaution? Might be either. I incline myself to the first supposition.'

Mrs Hubbard nodded emphatically.

'Whoever it was may have followed her here, perhaps listening outside the door. Then came in to stop Pat from going on.'

'And then—?'

Sharpe's face darkened. 'That person went back to Patricia's room with her, talking quite normally and easily. Perhaps Patricia taxed her with removing the bicarbonate and perhaps the other gave a plausible explanation.'

Mrs Hubbard said sharply:

'Why do you say "*her*"?'

'Funny thing—a pronoun! When we found the body, Nigel Chapman said, "I'll kill whoever did this. I'll kill *him*." *Him*," you notice. Nigel Chapman clearly believed the murder was done by a *man*. It may be because he associated the idea of violence with a man. It may be that he's got some particular suspicion pointing to a man, to some particular man. If the latter, we must find out his reasons for thinking so. But speaking for myself, I plump for a woman.'

'Why?'

'Just this. Somebody went into Patricia's room with her —someone with whom she felt quite at home. That points to another girl. The men don't go to the girls' bedroom doors unless it's for some special reason. That's right, isn't it, Mrs Hubbard?'

'Yes. It's not exactly a hard and fast rule, but it's fairly generally observed.'

'The other side of the house is cut off from this side, except on the ground floor. Taking it that the conversation earlier between Nigel and Pat was overheard, it would in all probability be a woman who overheard it.'

'Yes, I see what you mean. And some of the girls seem to spend half their time here listening at keyholes.'

She flushed and added apologetically:

'That's rather too harsh. Actually, although these houses are solidly built, they've been cut up and partitioned, and all the new work is flimsy as anything, like paper. You can't help hearing through it. Jean, I must admit, does do a good deal of snooping. She's the type. And of course, when Genevieve heard Nigel telling Pat his father had murdered his mother, she stopped and listened for all she was worth.'

The inspector nodded. He had listened to the evidence of Sally Finch and Jean Tomlinson and Genevieve. He said:

'Who occupies the rooms on either side of Patricia's?'

'Genevieve's is beyond it—but that's a good original wall. Elizabeth Johnston's is on the other side, nearer the stairs. That's only a partition wall.'

'That narrows it down a bit,' said the inspector.

'The French girl heard the *end* of the conversation, Sally Finch was present earlier on *before* she went out to post her letter. But the fact that those two girls *were* there automatically excludes anybody else having been able to snoop except for a very short period. Always with the exception of Elizabeth Johnston, who could have heard everything through the partition wall if she'd been in her bedroom but it seems to be fairly clear that she was already in the common-room when Sally Finch went out to the post.'

'She did not remain in the common-room all the time?'

'No, she went upstairs again at some period to fetch a book she had forgotten. As usual, nobody can say *when*.'

'It might have been any of them,' said Mrs Hubbard helplessly.

'As far as their statements go, yes—but we've got a little extra evidence.'

He took a small folded paper packet out of his pocket.

'What's that?' demanded Mrs Hubbard.

Sharpe smiled.

'A couple of hairs—I took them from between Patricia Lane's fingers.'

'You mean that—'

There was a tap on the door.

'Come in,' said the inspector.

The door opened to admit Mr Akibombo. He was smiling broadly, all over his black face.

'Please,' he said.

Inspector Sharpe said impatiently:

'Yes, Mr—er—um, what is it?'

'I think, please, I have statement to make. Of first-class importance to elucidation of sad and tragic occurrence.'

CHAPTER EIGHTEEN

'Now, Mr Akibombo,' said Inspector Sharpe, resignedly, 'let's hear, please, what all this is about.'

Mr Akibombo had been provided with a chair. He sat facing the others who were all looking at him with keen attention.

'Thank you. I begin now?'

'Yes, please.'

'Well, it is, you see, that sometimes I have the disquieting sensations in my stomach.'

'Oh.'

'Sick to my stomach. That is what Miss Sally calls it. But I am not, you see, actually *sick*. I do not, that is, vomit.'

Inspector Sharpe restrained himself with difficulty while these medical details were elaborated.

'Yes, yes,' he said. 'Very sorry, I'm sure. But you want to tell us—'

'It is, perhaps, unaccustomed food. I feel very full *here*.' Mr Akibombo indicated exactly where. 'I think myself, not enough meat, and too much what you call cardohydrates.'

'Carbohydrates,' the inspector corrected him mechanically. 'But I don't see—'

'Sometimes I take small pill, soda mint; and sometimes stomach powder. It does not matter very much *what* it is —so that a great pouf comes and much air—like *this*.' Mr Akibombo gave a most realistic and gigantic belch. 'After that,' he smiled seraphically, 'I feel much better, much better.'

The inspector's face was becoming a congested purple. Mrs Hubbard said authoritatively:

'We understand all about *that*. Now get on to the next part.'

'Yes. Certainly. Well, as I say, this happens to me early last week—I do not remember exactly which day. Very good macaroni and I eat a lot, and afterwards feel very bad. I try to do work for my professor but difficult to think with fullness here.' (Again Akibombo indicated the spot.) 'It is after supper in the common-room and only Elizabeth there and I say to her, "Have you bicarbonate or stomach powder, I have finished mine." And she says, "No. But," she says, "I saw some in Pat's drawer when I was putting back a handkerchief I borrowed from her. I will get it for you," she says. "Pat will not mind." So she goes upstairs and comes back with soda bicarbonate bottle. Very little left, at bottom of bottle, almost empty. I thank her and go with it to the bathroom, and I put nearly all of it about a teaspoonful in water and stir it up and drink it.'

'A *teaspoonful*? A teaspoonful! My God!'

The inspector gazed at him fascinated. Sergeant Cobb leaned forward with an astonished face. Mrs Hubbard said obscurely:

'Rasputin!'

'You swallowed a teaspoonful of *morphia*?'

'Naturally, I think it is bicarbonate.'

'Yes, yes, what I can't understand is why you're sitting here now!'

'And then, afterwards, I was ill, but really ill. Not just the fullness. Pain, bad pain in my stomach.'

'I can't make out why you're not dead!'

'Rasputin,' said Mrs Hubbard. 'They used to give him poison again and again, lots of it, and it didn't kill him!'

Mr Akibombo was continuing.

'So then, next day, when I am better, I take the bottle and the tiny bit of powder that is left in it to a chemist and I say please tell me what is this I have taken that has made me feel so bad?'

'Yes?'

'And he says come back later, and when I do, he says, "No wonder! This is *not* the bicarbonate. It is the borass—eek. The acid borasseek. You can put it in the eyes, yes, but if you swallow a teaspoonful it makes you ill."'

'Boracic?' The inspector stared at him stupefied. 'But how did boracic get into that bottle? What happened to the morphia?' He groaned, 'Of all the haywire cases!'

'And I have been thinking, please,' went on Akibombo.

'You have been thinking,' Sharpe said. 'And what have you been thinking?'

'I have been thinking of Miss Celia and how she died and that someone, after she was dead, must have come into her room and left there the empty morphia bottle and the little piece of paper that say she killed herself—'

Akibombo paused and the inspector nodded.

'And so I say—who could have done that? And I think if it is one of the girls it will be easy, but if a man not so easy, because he would have to go downstairs in our house and up the other stairs and someone might wake up and hear him or see him. So I think again, and I say, suppose it is someone in our house, but in the next room to Miss Celia's—only she is in this house, you understand? Outside his window is a balcony and outside hers is a balcony too, and she will sleep with her window open because that is hygienic practice. So if he is big and strong and athletic he could jump across.'

'The room next to Celia's in the other house,' said Mrs Hubbard. 'Let me see, that's Nigel's and—and . . .'

'Len Bateson's,' said the inspector. His finger touched the folded paper in his hand. 'Len Bateson.'

'He is very nice, yes,' said Mr Akibombo sadly. 'And to me most pleasant, but psychologically one does not know what goes on below top surface. That is so, is it not? That is modern theory. Mr Chandra Lal very angry when his boracic for the eyes disappears and later, when I ask, he says he has been told that it was taken by Len Bateson. . . .'

'The morphia was taken from Nigel's drawer and boracic was substituted for it, and then Patricia Lane came along and substituted soda bicarbonate for what she thought was morphia but which was really boracic powder. . . . Yes . . . I see . . .'

'I have helped you, yes?' Mr Akibombo asked politely.

'Yes, indeed, we're most grateful to you. Don't—er—repeat any of this.'

'No, sir. I will be most careful.'

Mr Akibombo bowed politely to all and left the room.

'Len Bateson,' said Mrs Hubbard, in a distressed voice. 'Oh! *No.*'

Sharpe looked at her.

'You don't want it to be Len Bateson?'

'I've got fond of that boy. He's got a temper, I know, but he's always seemed so *nice.*'

'That's been said about a lot of criminals,' said Sharpe.

Gently he unfolded his little paper packet. Mrs Hubbard obeyed his gesture and leaned forward to look.

On the white paper were two red short curly hairs. . . .

'Oh! dear,' said Mrs Hubbard.

'Yes,' said Sharpe reflectively. 'In my experience a murderer usually makes at least *one* mistake.'

'But it is beautiful, my friend,' said Hercule Poirot with admiration. 'So clear—so beautifully clear.'

'You sound as if you were talking about soup,' grumbled the inspector. 'It may be Consommé to you—but to me there's a good deal of thick Mock Turtle about it still.'

'Not now. Everything fits in in its appointed place.'

'Even these?'

As he had done to Mrs Hubbard, Inspector Sharpe produced his exhibit of two red hairs.

Poirot's answer was almost in the same words as Sharpe had used.

'Ah—yes,' he said. 'What do you call it on the radio? The one deliberate mistake.'

The eyes of the two men met.

'No one,' said Hercule Poirot, 'is as clever as they think they are.'

Inspector Sharpe was greatly tempted to say:

'Not even Hercule Poirot?' but he restrained himself.

'For the other, my friend, it is all fixed?'

'Yes, the balloon goes up to-morrow.'

'You go yourself?'

'No, I'm scheduled to appear at 26 Hickory Road. Cobb will be in charge.'

'We will wish him good luck.'

Gravely, Hercule Poirot raised his glass. It contained crème de menthe.

Inspector Sharpe raised his whisky glass.

'Here's hoping,' he said.

II

'They do think up things, these places,' said Sergeant Cobb.

He was looking with grudging admiration at the display window of SABRINA FAIR. Framed and enclosed in an expensive illustration of the glassmaker's art—the 'glassy green translucent wave'—Sabrina was displayed recumbent, clad in brief and exquisite panties and happily surrounded with every variety of deliciously packaged cosmetics. Besides the panties she wore various examples of barbaric costume jewellery.

Detective-Constable McCrae gave a snort of deep disapproval.

'Blasphemy, I call it. Sabrina Fair, that's Milton, that is.'

'Well, Milton isn't the Bible, my lad.'

'You'll not deny that Paradise Lost is about Adam and Eve and the garden of Eden and all the devils of hell and if that's not religion, what is?'

Sergeant Cobb did not enter on these controversial matters. He marched boldly into the establishment, the dour constable at his heels. In the shell pink interior of Sabrina Fair the sergeant and his satellite looked as out of place as the traditional bull in a china shop.

An exquisite creature in delicate salmon pink swam up to them, her feet hardly seeming to touch the floor.

Sergeant Cobb said, 'Good morning, madam,' and produced his credentials. The lovely creature withdrew in a flutter. An equally lovely but slightly older creature appeared. She in turn gave way to a superb and resplendent duchess whose blue grey hair and smooth cheeks set age and wrinkles at nought. Appraising steel grey eyes met the steady gaze of Sergeant Cobb.

'This is most unusual,' said the duchess severely. 'Please come this way.'

She led him through a square salon with a centre table where magazines and periodicals were heaped carelessly. All round the walls were curtained recesses where glimpses could be obtained of recumbent women supine under the ministrant hands of pink robed priestesses.

The duchess led the police officers into a small businesslike apartment with a big roll top desk, severe chairs, and no softening of the harsh northern light.

'I am Mrs Lucas, the proprietress of this establishment,' she said. 'My partner, Miss Hobhouse, is not here to-day.'

'No, madam,' said Sergeant Cobb, to whom this was no news.

'This search warrant of yours seems to be most high-handed,' said Mrs Lucas. 'This is Miss Hobhouse's private office. I sincerely hope that it will not be necessary for you to—er—upset our clients in any way.'

'I don't think you need to worry unduly on that score,' said Cobb. 'What we're after isn't likely to be in the public rooms.'

He waited politely until she unwillingly withdrew. Then he looked round Valerie Hobhouse's office. The narrow window gave a view of the back premises of other Mayfair firms. The walls were panelled in pale grey and there were two good Persian rugs on the floor. His eyes went from the small wall safe to the big desk.

'Won't be in the safe,' said Cobb. 'Too obvious.'

A quarter of an hour later, the safe and the drawers of the desk had yielded up their secrets.

'Looks like it's maybe a mare's nest,' said McCrae, who was by nature both gloomy and disapproving.

'We're only beginning,' said Cobb.

Having emptied the drawers of their contents and arranged the latter neatly in piles, he now proceeded to take the drawers out and turn them upside down.

He uttered an ejaculation of pleasure.

'Here we are, my lad,' he said.

Fastened to the underneath side of the bottom drawer with adhesive tape were a half-dozen small dark blue books with gilt lettering.

'Passports,' said Sergeant Cobb. 'Issued by Her Majesty's Secretary of State for Foreign Affairs, God bless his trusting heart.'

McCrae bent over with interest as Cobb opened the passports and compared the affixed photographs.

'Hardly think it was the same woman, would you?' said McCrae.

The passports were those of Mrs da Silva, Miss Irene

French, Mrs Olga Kohn, Miss Nina Le Mesurier, Mrs Gladys Thomas, and Miss Moira O'Neele. They represented a dark young woman whose age varied between twenty-five and forty.

'It's the different hair-do every time that does it,' said Cobb. 'Pompadour, curls. straight cut, page boy bob, etc. She's done something to her nose for Olga Kohn, plumpers in her cheeks for Mrs Thomas. Here are two more—foreign passports—Madame Mahmoudi, Algerian. Sheila Donovan, Eire. I'll say she's got bank accounts in all these different names.'

'Bit complicated, isn't that?'

'It has to be complicated, my lad. Inland Revenue always snooping round asking embarrassing questions. It's not so difficult to make money by smuggling goods—but it's hell and all to account for money when you've got it! I bet this little gambling club in Mayfair was started by the lady for just that reason. Winning money by gambling is about the only thing an income tax inspector can't check up on. A good part of the loot, I should say, is cached around in Algerian and French banks and in Eire. The whole thing's a thoroughly well thought out business-like set up. And then, one day, she must have had one of these fake passports lying about at Hickory Road and that poor little devil Celia saw it.'

CHAPTER TWENTY

'It was a clever idea of Miss Hobhouse's,' said Inspector Sharpe. His voice was indulgent, almost fatherly.

He shuffled the passports from one hand to the other like a man dealing cards.

'Complicated thing, finance,' he said. 'We've had a busy time haring round from one bank to the other. She covered her tracks well—her financial tracks, I mean. I'd say that in a couple of years' time she could have cleared out, gone abroad and lived happily ever after, as they say, on ill-gotten gains. It wasn't a big show—illicit diamonds, sapphires, etc., coming in—stolen stuff going out—and narcotics on the side, as you might say. Thoroughly well organised. She went abroad under her own and under different names, but never too often, and the actual smuggling was always done, unknowingly, by someone else. She had agents abroad who saw to the exchange of rucksacks at the right moment. Yes, it was a clever idea. And we've got M. Poirot here to thank for putting us on to it. It was smart of her, too, to suggest that psychological stealing stunt to poor little Miss Austin. You were wise to that almost at once, weren't you, M. Poirot?'

Poirot smiled in a deprecating manner and Mrs Hubbard looked admiringly at him. The conversation was strictly off the record in Mrs Hubbard's sitting-room.

'Greed was her undoing,' said Poirot. 'She was tempted by that fine diamond in Patricia Lane's ring. It was foolish of her because it suggested at once that she was used to handling precious stones—that business of prising the diamond out and replacing it with a zircon. Yes, that certainly gave me ideas about Valerie Hobhouse. She was clever, though, when I taxed her with inspiring Celia, she admitted it and explained it in a thoroughly sympathetic way.'

'But murder!' said Mrs Hubbard. 'Cold-blooded murder. I can't really believe it even now.'

Inspector Sharpe looked gloomy.

'We aren't in a position to charge her with the murder of Celia Austin yet,' he said. 'We've got her cold on the smuggling, of course. No difficulties about that. But the murder charge is more tricky. The public prosecutor doesn't see his way. There's motive, of course, and opportunity. She probably knew all about the bet and Nigel's possession of morphia, but there's no real evidence, and there are the two other deaths to take into account. She could have poisoned Mrs Nicoletis all right—but on the other hand, she definitely did not kill Patricia Lane. Actually she's about the only person who's completely in the clear. Geronimo says positively that she left the house at six o'clock. He sticks to that. I don't know whether she bribed him—'

'No,' said Poirot, shaking his head. 'She did not bribe him.'

'And we've the evidence of the chemist at the corner of the road. He knows her quite well and he sticks to it that she came in at five minutes past six and bought face powder and aspirin and used the telephone. She left his shop at quarter-past six and took a taxi from the rank outside.'

Poirot sat up in his chair.

'But that,' he said, 'is magnificent! It is just what we want!'

'What on earth do you mean?'

'I mean that she actually telephoned from the box at the chemist's shop.'

Inspector Sharpe looked at him in an exasperated fashion.

'Now, see here, M. Poirot. Let's take the known facts. At eight minutes past six, Patricia Lane is alive and telephoning to the police station from this room. You agree to that?'

'I do not think she was telephoning from this room.'

'Well then, from the hall downstairs.'

'Not from the hall either.'

Inspector Sharpe sighed.

'I suppose you don't deny that a call *was* put through to the police station? You don't think that I and my sergeant and Police-Constable Nye and Nigel Chapman were the victims of mass hallucination?'

'Assuredly not. A call was put through to you. I should say at a guess that it was put through from the public call-box at the chemist's on the corner.'

Inspector Sharpe's jaw dropped for a moment.

'You mean that *Valerie Hobhouse* put through that call? That she pretended to speak as Patricia Lane, and that Patricia Lane was *already dead*.'

'That is what I mean, yes.'

The inspector was silent for a moment, then he brought down his fist with a crash on the table.

'I don't believe it. The voice—I heard it myself—'

'You heard it, yes. A girl's voice—breathless, agitated. But you didn't know Patricia Lane's voice well enough to say definitely that it *was* her voice.'

'*I* didn't, perhaps. But it was Nigel Chapman who actually took the call. You can't tell me that Nigel Chapman could be deceived. It isn't so easy to disguise a voice over the telephone, or to counterfeit somebody else's voice. Nigel Chapman would have known if it wasn't Pat's voice speaking.'

'Yes,' said Poirot. '*Nigel Chapman would have known.* Nigel Chapman knew quite well that it *wasn't* Patricia. Who should know better than he, since he had killed her with a blow on the back of the head only a short while before.'

It was a moment or two before the inspector recovered his voice.

'Nigel Chapman? Nigel Chapman? But when we found her dead—he cried—cried like a child.'

'I dare say,' said Poirot. 'I think he was as fond of that girl as he could be of anybody—but that wouldn't save her—not if she represented a menace to his interests. All along, Nigel Chapman has stood out as the obvious probability. Who had morphia in his possession? Nigel Chapman. Who had the shallow brilliant intellect to plan, and the audacity to carry out fraud and murder? Nigel Chapman. Who do we know to be both ruthless and vain? Nigel Chapman. He has all the hallmarks of the killer; the

overweening vanity, the spitefulness, the growing reckless-
ness that led him to draw attention to himself in every con-
ceivable way—using the green ink in a stupendous double
bluff, and finally overreaching himself by the silly deliberate mistake of putting Len Bateson's hairs in Patricia's
fingers, oblivious of the fact that as Patricia was struck
down from behind, she could not possibly have grasped her
assailant by the hair. They are like that, these murderers,
carried away by their own egoism, by their admiration of
their own cleverness, relying on their charm—for he *has*
charm, this Nigel—he has all the charm of a spoiled child
who has never grown up, who never will grow up—who
sees only one thing, himself, and what he wants!'

'But why, M. Poirot? Why murder? Celia Austin, perhaps, but why Patricia Lane?'

'That,' said Poirot, 'we have got to find out.'

CHAPTER TWENTY-ONE

'I haven't seen you for a long time,' said old Mr Endicott to Hercule Poirot. He peered at the other keenly. 'It's very nice of you to drop in.'

'Not really,' said Hercule Poirot. 'I want something.'

'Well, as you know, I'm deeply in your debt. You cleared up that nasty Abernethy business for me.'

'I am surprised really to find you here. I thought you had retired.'

The old lawyer smiled grimly. His firm was a most respectable and old-established one.

'I came in specially to-day to see a very old client. I still attend to the affairs of one or two old friends.'

'Sir Arthur Stanley was an old friend and client, was he not?'

'Yes. We've undertaken all his legal work since he was quite a young man. A very brilliant man, Poirot—quite an exceptional brain.'

'His death was announced on the six o'clock news yesterday, I believe.'

'Yes. The funeral's on Friday. He's been ailing some time. A malignant growth, I understand.'

'Lady Stanley died some years ago?'

'Two and a half years ago, roughly.'

The keen eyes below the bushy brows looked sharply at Poirot.

'How did she die?'

The lawyer replied promptly.

'Overdose of sleeping stuff. Medinal as far as I remember.'

'There was an inquest?'

'Yes. The verdict was that she took it accidentally.'

'Did she?'

Mr Endicott was silent for a moment.

'I won't insult you,' he said. 'I've no doubt you've got a

good reason for asking. Medinal's a rather dangerous drug
I understand, because there's not a big margin between
an effective dose and a lethal one. If the patient gets drowsy
and forgets she's taken a dose and takes another—well, it
can have a fatal result.'

Poirot nodded.

'Is that what she did?'

'Presumably. There was no suggestion of suicide, or
suicidal tendencies.'

'And no suggestion of—anything else?'

Again that keen glance was shot at him.

'Her husband gave evidence.'

'And what did he say?'

'He made it clear that she did sometimes get confused
after taking her nightly dose and ask for another.'

'Was he lying?'

'Really, Poirot, what an outrageous question. Why should
you suppose for a minute that I should know?'

Poirot smiled. The attempt at bluster did not deceive him

'I suggest, my friend, that you know very well. But for
the moment I will not embarrass you by asking you what
you know. Instead I will ask you for an opinion. The
opinion of one man about another. Was Arthur Stanley the
kind of man who would do away with his wife if he wanted
to marry another woman.'

Mr Endicott jumped as though he had been stung by a
wasp.

'Preposterous,' he said angrily. 'Quite preposterous. And
there was no other woman. Stanley was devoted to his wife.'

'Yes,' said Poirot. 'I thought so. And now—I will come
to the purpose of my call upon you. You are the solicitors
who drew up Arthur Stanley's will. You are, perhaps, his
executor.'

'That is so.'

'Arthur Stanley had a son. The son quarrelled with his
father at the time of his mother's death. Quarrelled with
him and left home. He even went so far as to change his
name.'

'That I did not know. What's he calling himself?'

'We shall come to that. Before we do I am going to make an assumption. If I am right, perhaps you will admit the fact. I think that Arthur Stanley left a sealed letter with you, a letter to be opened under certain circumstances or after his death.'

'Really, Poirot! In the Middle Ages you would certainly have been burnt at the stake. How you can possibly know the things you do!'

'I am right then? I think there was an alternative in the letter. Its contents were either to be destroyed—or you were to take a certain course of action.'

He paused. The other did not speak.

'*Bon dieu!*' said Poirot, with alarm. 'You have not already destroyed—'

He broke off in relief as Mr Endicott slowly shook his head in negation.

'We never act in haste,' he said reprovingly. 'I have to make full inquiries—to satisfy myself absolutely—'

He paused. 'This matter,' he said severely, 'is highly confidential. Even to you, Poirot—' He shook his head.

'And if I show you good cause why you should speak.'

'That is up to you. I cannot conceive how you can possibly know anything at all that is relevant to the matter we are discussing.'

'I do not *know*—so I have to guess. If I guess correctly—'

'Highly unlikely,' said Mr Endicott, with a wave of his hand.

Poirot drew a deep breath.

'Very well then. It is in my mind that your instructions are as follows. In the event of Sir Arthur's death, you are to trace his son Nigel, to ascertain where he is living and how he is living and particularly whether he is or has been engaged in any criminal activity whatsoever.'

This time Mr Endicott's impregnable legal calm was really shattered. He uttered an exclamation such as few had ever heard from his lips.

'Since you appear to be in full possession of the facts,' he said, 'I'll tell you anything you want to know. I gather you've come across young Nigel in the course of your professional activities. What's the young devil been up to?'

'I think the story goes as follows. After he had left home he changed his name, telling anyone who was interested that he had to do so as a condition of a legacy. He then fell in with some people who were running a smuggling racket—drugs and jewels. I think it was due to him that the racket assumed its final form—an exceedingly clever one involving the using of innocent *bona fide* students. The whole thing was operated by two people, Nigel Chapman, as he now called himself, and a young woman called Valerie Hobhouse who, I think, originally introduced him to the smuggling trade. It was a small private concern and they worked it on a commission basis—but it was immensely profitable. The goods had to be of small bulk, but thousands of pounds worth of gems and narcotics occupy a very small space. Everything went well until one of those unforeseen chances occurred. A police officer came one day to a students' hostel to make inquiries in connection with a murder near Cambridge. I think you know the reason why that particular piece of information should cause Nigel to panic. He thought the police were after *him*. He removed certain electric light bulbs so that the light should be dim and he also, in a panic, took a certain rucksack out into the back yard, hacked it to pieces and threw it behind the boiler since he feared traces of narcotic might be found in its false bottom.

'His panic was quite unfounded—the police had merely come to ask questions about a certain Eurasian student—but one of the girls living in the hostel had happened to look out of her window and had seen him destroying the rucksack. That did not immediately sign her death warrant. Instead, a clever scheme was thought up by which she herself was induced to commit certain foolish actions which would place her in a very invidious position. But they carried that scheme too far. I was called in. I advised going to the police. The girl lost her head and confessed. She confessed, that is, to the things that *she* had done. But she went, I think, to Nigel, and urged him to confess also to the rucksack business and to spilling ink over a fellow

184

student's work. Neither Nigel nor his accomplice could consider attention being called to the rucksack—their whole plan of campaign would be ruined. Moreover Celia, the girl in question, had another dangerous piece of knowledge which she revealed, as it happened, the night I dined there. She knew who Nigel really was.'

'But surely—' Mr Endicott frowned.

'Nigel had moved from one world to another. Any former friends he met might know that he now called himself Chapman, but they knew nothing of what he was doing. In the hostel nobody knew that his real name was Stanley—but Celia suddenly revealed that she knew him in both capacities. She also knew that Valerie Hobhouse, on one occasion at least, had travelled abroad on a false passport. She knew too much. The next evening she went out to meet him by appointment somewhere. He gave her a drink of coffee and in it was morphia. She died in her sleep with everything arranged to look like suicide.'

Mr Endicott stirred. An expression of deep distress crossed his face. He murmured something under his breath.

'But that was not the end,' said Poirot. 'The woman who owned the chain of hostels and students' clubs died soon after in suspicious circumstances and then, finally, there came the last most cruel and heartless crime. Patricia Lane, a girl who was devoted to Nigel and of whom he himself was really fond, meddled unwittingly in his affairs, and moreover insisted that he should be reconciled to his father before the latter died. He told her a string of lies, but he realised that her obstinacy might urge her actually to write a second letter after the first was destroyed. I think, my friend, that you can tell me why, from his point of view, that would have been such a fatal thing to happen.'

Mr Endicott rose. He went across the room to a safe, unlocked it, and came back with a long envelope in his hand. It had a broken red seal on the back of it. He drew out two enclosures and laid them before Poirot.

DEAR ENDICOTT,

You will open this after I am dead. I wish you to

trace my son Nigel and find out if he has been guilty of any criminal actions whatsoever.

The facts I am about to tell you are known to me only. Nigel has always been profoundly unsatisfactory in his character. He has twice been guilty of forging my name to a cheque. On each occasion I acknowledged the signature as mine, but warned him that I would not do so again. On the third occasion it was his mother's name he forged. She charged him with it. He begged her to keep silence. She refused. She and I had discussed him, and she made it clear she was going to tell me. It was then, in handing her her evening sleeping mixture, he administered an overdose. Before it took effect, however, she had come to my room and told me all about matters. When, the next morning, she was found dead, I knew who had done it.

I accused Nigel and told him that I intended to make a clean breast of all the facts to the police. He pleaded desperately with me. What would you have done, Endicott? I have no illusions about my son, I know him for what he is, one of those dangerous misfits who have neither conscience nor pity. I had no cause to save him. But it was the thought of my beloved wife that swayed me. Would *she* wish me to execute justice? I thought that I knew the answer—she would have wanted her son saved from the scaffold. She would have shrunk, as I shrank, from the dragging down of our name. But there was another consideration. I firmly believe that once a killer, always a killer. There might be, in the future, other victims. I made a bargain with my son, and whether I did right or wrong, I do not know. He was to write out a confession of his crime which I should keep. He was to leave my house and never return, but make a new life for himself. I would give him a second chance. Money belonging to his mother would come to him automatically. He had had a good education. He had every chance of making good.

But—if he were convicted of any criminal activity whatsoever the confession he had left with me should go to the police. I safeguarded myself by explaining that my own death would not solve the problem.

You are my oldest friend. I am placing a burden on your shoulders, but I ask it in the name of a dead woman who was also your friend. Find Nigel. If his record is clean, destroy this letter and the enclosed confession. If not—then justice must be done.

Your affectionate friend,
ARTHUR STANLEY

'Ah!' Poirot breathed a long sigh.
He unfolded the enclosure.

I hereby confess that I murdered my mother by giving her an overdose of medinal on November 18, 195—

NIGEL STANLEY

CHAPTER TWENTY-TWO

'You quite understand your position, Miss Hobhouse. I have already warned you—'

Valerie Hobhouse cut him short.

'I know what I'm doing. You've warned me that what I say will be used in evidence. I'm prepared for that. You've got me on the smuggling charge. I haven't got a hope. That means a long term of imprisonment. This other means that I'll be charged as an accessory to murder.'

'Your being willing to make a statement may help you, but I can't make any promise or hold out any inducement.'

'I don't know that I care. Just as well end it all as languish in prison for years. I want to make a statement. I may be what you call an accessory, but I'm not a killer. I never intended murder or wanted it. I'm not such a fool. What I do want is that there should be a clear case against Nigel. . . .

'Celia knew far too much, but I could have dealt with that somehow. Nigel didn't give me time. He got her to come out and meet him, told her that he was going to own up to the rucksack and the ink business and then slipped her the morphia in a cup of coffee. He'd got hold of her letter to Mrs Hubbard earlier on and had torn out a useful "suicide" phrase. He put that and the empty morphia phial (which he had retrieved after pretending to throw it away) by her bed. I see now that he'd been contemplating murder for quite a little time. Then he came and told me what he'd done. For my own sake I had to stand in with him.

'The same thing must have happened with Mrs Nick. He'd found out that she drank, that she was getting un-reliable—he managed to meet her somewhere on her way home, and poisoned her drink. He denied it to me—but I know that that's what he did. Then came Pat. He came up to my room and told me what had happened. He told me what I'd got to do—so that both he and I would have an unbreakable alibi. I was in the net by then, there was no way out. . . . I suppose, if you hadn't caught me, I'd have got away abroad somewhere, and made a new life for myself. But you did catch me . . . And now I only care about one thing—to make sure that that cruel smiling devil gets hanged.'

Inspector Sharpe drew a deep breath. All this was eminently satisfactory, it was an unbelievable piece of luck; but he was puzzled.

The constable licked his pencil.

'I'm not sure that I quite understand,' began Sharpe.

She cut him short.

'You don't need to understand. I've got my reasons.'

Hercule Poirot spoke very gently.

'Mrs Nicoletis?' he asked.

He heard the sharp intake of her breath.

'She was—your mother, was she not?'

'Yes,' said Valerie Hobhouse. 'She was my mother . . .'

CHAPTER TWENTY-THREE

'I do not understand,' said Mr Akibombo plaintively.

He looked anxiously from one red head to the other.

Sally Finch and Len Bateson were conducting a conversation which Mr Akibombo found hard to follow.

'Do you think,' asked Sally, 'that Nigel meant *me* to be suspected, or *you*?'

'Either, I should say,' replied Len. 'I believe he actually took the hairs from *my* brush.'

'I do not understand, please,' said Mr Akibombo. 'Was it then Mr Nigel who jumped the balcony?'

'Nigel can jump like a cat. I couldn't have jumped across that space. I'm far too heavy.'

'I want to apologise very deeply and humbly for wholly unjustifiable suspicions.'

'That's all right,' said Len.

'Actually, you helped a lot,' said Sally. 'All your thinking—about the boracic.'

Mr Akibombo brightened up.

'One ought to have realised all along,' said Len, 'that Nigel was a thoroughly maladjusted type and—'

'Oh, for heaven's sake—you sound just like Colin. Frankly, Nigel always gave me the creeps—and at last I see why. Do you realise, Len, that if poor Sir Arthur Stanley hadn't been sentimental and had turned Nigel straight over to the police, three other people would be alive to-day? It's a solemn thought.'

'Still, one can understand what he felt about it—'

'Please, Miss Sally.'

'Yes, Akibombo?'

'If you meet my professor at University party to-night will you tell him, please, that I have done some good thinking? My professor he says often that I have a muddled thought process.'

'I'll tell him,' said Sally.

Len Bateson was looking the picture of gloom.

'In a week's time you'll be back in America,' he said.

There was a momentary silence.

'I shall come back,' said Sally. 'Or you might come and do a course over there.'

'What's the use?'

'Akibombo,' said Sally, 'would you like, one day, to be best man at a wedding?'

'What is best man, please?'

'The bridegroom, Len here for instance, gives you a ring to keep for him, and he and you go to church very smartly dressed and at the right moment he asks you for the ring and you give it to him, and he puts it on my finger, and the organ plays the wedding march and everybody cries. And there we are.'

'You mean that you and Mr Len are to be married?'

'That's the idea.'

'Sally!'

'Unless, of course, Len doesn't care for the idea.'

'Sally! But you don't know—about my father—'

'So what? Of course I know. So your father's nuts. All right, so are lots of people's fathers.'

'It isn't a hereditary type of mania. I can assure you of that, Sally. If you only knew how desperately unhappy I've been about you.'

'I did just have a tiny suspicion.'

'In Africa,' said Mr Akibombo, 'in old days, before atomic age and scientific thought had come, marriage customs very curious and interesting. I tell you—'

'You'd better not,' said Sally. 'I have an idea they might make both Len and me blush, and when you've got red hair it's very noticeable when you blush.'

II

Hercule Poirot signed the last of the letters that Miss Lemon had laid before him.

'*Très bien*,' he said gravely. 'Not a single mistake.'

Miss Lemon looked slightly affronted.

'I don't often make mistakes, I hope,' she said.

'Not often. But it has happened. How is your sister, by the way?'

'She is thinking of going on a cruise, M. Poirot. To the northern capitals.'

'Ah,' said Hercule Poirot.

He wondered if—possibly—on a cruise—?

Not that he himself would undertake a sea voyage—not for any inducement. . . .

The clock behind him struck one.

> '*The clock struck one,*
> *The mouse ran down*
> *Hickory, dickory, dock,*'

declared Hercule Poirot.

'I beg your pardon, M. Poirot?'

'Nothing,' said Hercule Poirot.